W9-BUG-937

WIFE: BOUGHT
AND PAID FOR

WIFE: BOUGHT AND PAID FOR

BY

JACQUELINE BAIRD

First published in Great Britain 2002
Large Print edition 2003
Harlequin Mills & Boon Limited,
Eton House, 18-24 Paradise Road,
Richmond, Surrey TW9 1SR

© Jacqueline Baird 2002

ISBN 0 263 17884 6

Set in Times Roman 16½ on 18 pt.
16-0303-51285

Printed and bound in Great Britain
by Antony Rowe Ltd, Chippenham, Wiltshire

PROLOGUE

PENNY ran lightly across the field, leapt over the fence into the old stable yard, and headed straight for the back door of the house. She was late and Veronica would kill her. Penny had promised to return before five to babysit her half-brother, while her stepmother went to the hairdresser. But her boss in the antique shop had been late getting back, and then Penny had bumped into her best friend, Jane Turner, the local vicar's daughter, and Jane's brother Simon.

Simon had just returned from a trekking holiday in the Himalayas. A year older than the girls, he was full of his experiences, and waxed lyrical about his prowess as a mountain climber. Jane was delighted because her older sister Patricia, who was married and lived in New York, was coming home on holiday next month, and bringing her new baby with her.

5

Penny was pleased for her friends but it had delayed her even more.

'Sorry, sorry,' Penny yelled as she dashed into the rear porch that led to the kitchen.

Veronica stood, baby James in her arms, blocking her way. 'About time! I'm going to be late and you know how important this dinner is tonight. We have invited Mr Maffeiano and his PA, and with a bit of luck not only will Maffeiano buy the land, and solve our immediate money worries, but also he might be persuaded into going into business with Julian. It could be the making of your father, and heaven knows we need the income to keep this place up.'

It was the familiar moan, and Penny shrivelled a little inside. Veronica wasn't a bad person; in fact, when she had first married Penny's father Julian eighteen months ago they had got on well. It was only when Veronica had given birth to a baby boy ten months later, and begun talking of when James would inherit the estate, and her husband had disabused her of the notion, informing her Haversham

Park was always left to the oldest child, irrespective of sex, that she'd changed.

Penny's own mother had died of cancer when Penny was thirteen, and for a while her father had been depressed. But four years later he had met and married Veronica.

'Well, take him, for heaven's sake! I have to dash,' Veronica snapped.

'Sorry, Veronica,' Penny apologised again, reaching out and taking James into her arms. She adored her brother. But, casting a glance at her stepmother, she could not help thinking uncharitably that it was amazing how quickly Veronica had lost interest in Penny, and to some extent the baby, when she'd realised her husband wasn't as wealthy as she'd thought.

'Sorry isn't good enough—we really do need the money. Working in that dusty junk shop for a gap year before going to university will nowhere near cover the cost of keeping you at college for three more. Your father will have to pay. Heavens! We can't even afford a caterer! Feed James, and put him to bed, then keep an eye on Mrs Brown's cooking. The woman is far too old to work and she flatly refused to take James for me, saying she was too busy. The nerve of the woman.'

'Okay,' Penny agreed as Veronica swept out. Penny sighed with relief as she walked into the kitchen.

'She's gone and left you holding the baby again,' Mrs Brown, the live-in housekeeper, remarked grimly.

'I don't mind.' Penny grinned at the older woman and slipped a gurgling James into his high chair, then set about preparing his bottle and food.

''Brownie'', as Penny called her, had lived at Haversham Park since before Penny was born and Penny could not imagine the house without her. Much as Veronica complained about the woman, she had not tried to get rid of her.

However, this was probably because Brownie worked for a small salary and, more importantly, Veronica did not cook... In fact Veronica's one aim in life, as far as Penny could see, was to look good and be part of what she called the social scene. This apparently, entailed flitting back and forward to London for dinners and charity balls.

Penny grimaced; it was a ball that was responsible for tonight's dinner. Veronica had persuaded her father to take her to an exclusive charity event in London. As luck would have it, Veronica had bumped into an old friend of hers, a businessman, and had introduced him to Penny's father. One thing had led to another, and apparently the man was interested in purchasing land, perhaps for a golf course. Personally Penny could not see the point but, as her father had explained, there was no money in farming any more, and they needed money. Veronica was right; this was an ideal opportunity for Julian to make some money and her father almost always bowed to what Veronica wanted, Penny thought ruefully. Who could blame him? He was a man in his fifties with a beautiful young wife and he just wanted to keep her happy.

But Penny took heart in the fact they would still keep the home she loved, a stone-built Tudor-styled house set in five acres of parkland, and she began feeding James with a smile on her face.

Once he was fed and happy, Penny left James with Brownie and set the large oak table in the dining room with the finest damask cloth and silver cutlery. Then, with a brief glance at her wrist-watch she dashed back to the kitchen.

A sleepy James stretched out his arms to her and she swept him up in hers, giving him a cuddle and a kiss. 'Bed for you, little man,' she murmured, and strolled out into the hall. Her foot was on the bottom step when the front door was flung open. Penny stopped and turned. Veronica was back quick.

'Ah, Penelope and my favourite boy.' Her smiling father walked towards her.

Oh, my God! She stifled a groan. The guests had arrived early, over two hours early by Penny's reckoning!

Solo Maffeiano entered the hall, and wondered what the hell he was doing here. Two nights ago he had spent a couple of hours of inventive sex with Lisa, his occasional mistress in New

York. She was a lawyer, she knew the score and was very accommodating.

In a way it was her fault he was here now. On a previous date with Lisa months ago, he had been flicking through a year-old magazine while he'd waited to be picked up for the airport. The centre-fold picture of a wedding had attracted his attention: the marriage of Veronica Jones to a much older minor English aristocrat, Julian Haversham.

Solo had laughed out loud as he had known the lady seven years before, not in the biblical sense, but it had not been for the want of trying on her part. Veronica had been the girlfriend of an Arab business associate of his when they had spent a week cruising the Greek Islands. Bridal material she was not!

But the picture of the bridesmaid, the daughter of the groom, had caught his eye. The Honourable Penelope Haversham was a beauty, with pale blonde hair and milky white skin, and an innocent, almost fey quality about the small, slender figure that had intrigued him.

He had met Veronica and her new husband at a charity ball in London a couple of weeks back. Now following his PA Tina down the hall, he realised he should have taken her advice and had nothing to do with the proposition Veronica was pushing, the purchase of farming land and possibly a joint leisure development. If the house were included it might have been viable. But it would be sacrilege to alter it. It was a beautiful example of Tudor architecture, and Solo appreciated works of art. His hobby was collecting rare objects; his home in Italy was a treasure trove of *objets d'art*.

Probably because he had been brought up in the back streets of Naples with a whore for a grandmother and a mother who'd followed in the family tradition! He was the result of an American sailor's fling with his mother. He was named Saul after him but the name was quickly bastardised to Solo, and by the time he was ten he'd been on his own.

There was very little he had not seen and done. But blessed with a brilliant mind and a quick tongue, he had never fallen foul of the law. He had worked and acquired a formal education whenever he'd had the time and opportunity, ultimately graduating with honours in economics. But privately he acknowledged the economics of poverty and the street had proved to be a much more valuable lesson, when dealing with the upper echelons of international finance.

At thirty-four he was a success. Wealthy beyond most people's wildest dreams, he was a whiz at playing the markets and had also invested heavily in property around the world. He could have any woman he wanted without really trying. So why was he wasting his valuable time on the off chance of seeing the girl from the picture? He wondered, his lips twisting in a self-derogatory smile.

Then he saw her, and he stopped dead. The picture did not begin to do her justice.

Penny held James a little more securely and, putting a brave face on it, she said, 'You're early, Daddy. I'm just going to put James to bed.' Her father was a tall, slender man, with white hair and brown eyes, and she loved him to bits.

'Not to worry, darling. Come and let me introduce you to our guests.'

Penny's glance skimmed over two people. A redheaded woman and a tall man, half hidden behind her father.

'My daughter Penelope.' Her father stepped aside and smiled at the couple, before glancing back at Penny. 'Solo Maffeiano, and his PA Tina Jenson, our guests this evening. It was such a lovely afternoon we decided to come down early and conduct our business here rather than in a London office.'

The woman was tall and elegant. 'How do you do?' Penny said politely. 'I hope you will excuse me not shaking hands, but as you can see my arms are full.'

Penny looked up at the other guest with a polite smile on her face, and her heart quite inexplicably began thumping against her ribs. She simply stared, struck dumb by the sheer dynamic presence of the man.

Solo Maffeiano was the most devastatingly attractive man she had ever seen. He was wearing a tailored lightweight grey suit that fitted his elegant frame to perfection. He was well over six feet tall with wide shoulders that tapered down to lean hips and long legs. He was olive-skinned with thick black curling hair, his eyes were a piercing grey, his nose straight. His perfectly sculptured lips were curved in a smile over brilliant white teeth.

'Delighted to meet you, Penelope,' Solo husked. She was a vision of feminine perfection with a baby in her arms, and Solo felt an instant reaction in the groin area. It had not happened like that for him in years.

Her hair was fair, and it fell long and straight down her back like fine silk. Her petite features held a perfect symmetry, her lips full and sensually curved. Her eyes were a stunning green but darkening to deep jade as she watched him, the lashes thick and curling, and he noted the tinge of pink on her cheeks.

He knew the effect he had on women and for the most part ignored it, but he felt a stab of savage masculine pride that this dainty creature before him reacted so helplessly. In that instant he decided he wanted her, and he was a man who always got what he wanted.

Penny finally found her tongue. 'And you, Mr Maffeiano.' She swallowed hard.

'Please call me Solo.' He smiled again, and she was mesmerised.

'Solo,' she breathed his name, and at that moment young James decided he did not like his sister's attention diverted from himself, and grabbed a handful of her hair and tugged.

'Oh, you little devil,' she cried at the swift stab of pain, bringing her back to reality with a jolt, but she was grateful to James. It had stopped her staring at the man like a besotted fool. 'Come on, it's bed for you.' With the briefest glance at the others, she murmured, 'Excuse me.'

But before she could turn Solo Maffeiano reached out one elegant finger and slid it gently down James's chubby cheek.

'I hope you know how lucky you are, boy, with a beautiful girl to take you to bed.'

James gurgled happily and reached a chubby hand out to the man and the others all laughed. Penny shot a startled glance at the dark stranger, and blushed scarlet. She saw the knowing amusement lurking in his silver eyes; he knew exactly how he affected her. How he affected every woman he met, she thought, reality clicking in. He was a sophisticated, hand-some beast—add wealth and power, and he had it all. He was way out of her league, she told herself, turning to her father and gripping James like a lifeline.

'See you later, Daddy. Veronica is not back yet, and I must get James to bed.' She was babbling, she knew, but she needed to get away from Solo Maffeiano and the peculiar feelings, the tension he aroused in her. 'I'll see you all at dinner,' she said and almost ran up the stairs.

Lying in the bath later when James was safely tucked up in bed, Penny told herself she had overreacted. Solo Maffeiano was just a man like any other. It had been shock at the early arrival of the guests that had made her react so oddly.

It was almost eight when Penny made her way back downstairs. She had herself firmly under control—she was nearly nineteen. no longer a giddy teenager prone to blush if a boy so much as looked at her.

Her grin vanished as she walked into the drawing room for a pre-dinner drink.

Conversation stopped dead and four pairs of eyes turned to look at her.

'Really, Penny, you must learn to be punctual. I said seven-thirty for eight.' Veronica's opening comment had her stuttering for a response.

Her father's 'Leave the child alone, you know how Penny adores playing with James and she loses all track of time,' and brief smile before he looked around the other three did nothing for her self-esteem.

Tina Jenson smiled politely at Penny, and turned back to Solo Maffeiano.

But he simply ignored everyone else and crossed the room to Penny. His cool grey eyes flicked over the mass of fair hair she had swept up and knotted on top of her head, roamed down over her small face, her elegant neck and slender shoulders, and lingered on the boat neckline of her dress that revealed the soft curve of her surprisingly luscious breasts. His intent gaze dropped lower to the indentation of her waist, flat stomach, and down to where her straight skirt skimmed her slim hips and ended some two inches above her knees, right down to where her small feet were encased in high-heeled black sandals.

'You look beautiful, well worth waiting for,' he said with casual charm, taking her arm, 'And your father must be blind if he thinks you're a child,' he drawled huskily so only she could hear.

The touch of his fingers on her bare flesh seemed to burn through to the bone. Penny felt a wild heat surge through her body, and she did not know what had hit her.

Dinner was torture to Penny, although she persuaded Brownie to pretend her arthritis was bad so that Penny could do the serving.

Brownie gave her a quizzical look. 'Your stepmother won't like that.'

'Tough, I don't want to be stuck listening to boring business all night.'

A few minutes later Penny walked back into the dining room, carrying a tray, with the first course, melon and Parma ham.

'Where is Mrs Brown?' Veronica demanded curtly.

'Her arthritis is bothering her so I offered to help.'

'The trouble is good help is so hard to find when you live in a backwater like this,' Veronica began as Julian dealt with the wine.

Thirty miles or so outside Cambridge, the village was small, but it was also only about ninety minutes' drive into London, so hardly the back of beyond, Penny thought dryly as she put the plates on the table and took a seat next to Tina. Only then did Solo Maffeiano sit down directly facing her.

'I can imagine,' Tina Jenson drawled in agreement, while Penny kept her head down and tried to eat. 'But if Solo does decide to invest in the place I'm sure he will have no trouble finding staff. He never does,' Tina concluded with a smile at her boss.

Penny's head shot up at the words, and with a horrified glance at the man opposite, 'But the house is not for sale,' she blurted.

Solo leaned back in his chair, his silver gaze sweeping slowly over the delicate beauty of her features. He caught the tightening of her lush mouth, the tension she could not quite hide, before he captured her gaze with his own.

'Isn't that up to your father to decide?' he asked smoothly. 'After all, you're a very attractive young woman, some man is bound to snap you up before long.' One ebony brow arched enquiringly. 'Or are you already committed to some lucky man?'

Penelope heard her father's soft chuckle, and felt herself the object of all eyes around the table, and colour surged in her cheeks. 'No,' she responded quietly, 'to both your questions,' she concluded with a brief flare of resentment she could not quite disguise. Solo was deliberately needling her. She might be young, but she could recognise a chauvinistic statement when she heard one.

'Penelope is right,' Veronica piped up, supposedly in support of Penny, but then she went on to describe how Penelope stood to inherit the house. As Julian's wife Veronica only had the right to live in it, never own it, as did baby James.

Incredibly hurt by Veronica's implication that Penny was likely to throw her stepmother and brother out, she leapt to her feet, and whipped around the table collecting the plates.

It was some consolation to hear her father say firmly, 'That is not quite true Veronica, I could sell if I wanted to, but I don't. Havershams have lived here for three hundred years, and always will as far as I'm concerned. And I have not the least doubt Penelope would share everything with her family. We Havershams always do.'

Penelope slanted her father a grateful smile for sticking up for her, and shot off to the kitchen without another word.

For the rest of the meal she kept quiet and listened. But keeping her eyes from straying to the handsome man opposite was not such an easy feat. She couldn't help but look at him. Solo Maffeiano's voice was deep and melodious, his English had the slightest trace of an Italian accent, and his easy wit as the conversation flowed held her enthralled. But when Veronica started name-dropping shamelessly as she described the house party she and Julian were going to attend that weekend at Lord Somerton's, Penny had had enough.

She glimpsed the cynical smile on Solo Maffeiano's face, saw the contempt in his grey eyes, and she cringed. Looking down at the table, she placed her napkin by her plate before rising to her feet and declaring brightly to no one in particular, 'I'll go and get the coffee.' She couldn't get away fast enough.

'I'll help you,' Solo Maffeiano declared smoothly.

'No, no, please, you're a guest,' Penny flung over her shoulder as she scuttled out of the room and into the kitchen.

Breathing deeply, Penny crossed to the bench where the coffee percolator stood. Brownie had gone to bed, but she had left the tray, and the coffee on, bless her!

Not long now and Penny could make her own escape. She grasped the edge of the bench to steady her shaking nerves. What a meal! She had never felt so aware, so disturbed by a member of the opposite sex in her life. Solo Maffeiano had the power to make her heart shake with only a glance from his pale eyes, and she wasn't sure she liked it.

Sighing, she turned, only to freeze at the sight of the man in question strolling towards her. 'What are you doing here? I told you I don't need any help,' she snapped.

He didn't immediately answer. Instead he stopped and captured both her hands in his and very slowly folded them behind her back, bringing her into intimate contact with his tall frame. A shiver rippled through her as her breasts pressed against his broad chest, her slender legs trapped against the strength of hard, masculine thighs. She tried to wriggle free, then gasped as she felt the stirring of his mighty body and its blatant masculine sign of passion.

A mixture of innocent embarrassment and not so innocent helpless heated arousal caused a tide of pink to sweep up over her face. Penny stared up at him and was paralysed by the blinding flame of desire in his eyes, her heart hammering against her chest so hard she could hardly breathe. Nothing like this had ever happened to her before.

'What I have ached to do since the minute I set eyes on you,' Solo declared, and smiled a slow, soft curve of his firm mouth. His dark head bent and too late she realised the danger she was in.

'No,' Penny gasped at the same time as his mouth covered hers. She had been kissed before, not very often, and never like this, was her last conscious thought.

The sexy male scent of him filled her nostrils, a hot, liquid sensation flowed through her body making her breasts tingle, and heat pool at the junction of her thighs, and his mouth! His mouth moved on hers with a soft, sensual pleasure, his tongue darting between parted lips, gently then fiercely plundering the hot, sweet interior in an erotic, wonderful kiss that quickly flared out of control.

Solo groaned and, freeing her hands, he slipped his own firmly around her waist, holding her in intimate contact with his hard body.

Penny felt his other hand sweep up under her breasts and cup the aching fullness in his palm. Her slender body arched into him as his thumb stroked across the tip of her breast, bringing the tender nipple into a rigid peak against the fabric of her dress. 'Don't.' Her voice was a shocked murmur, verging on a moan.

Solo lifted his head, taking a swift breath. *Dio!* The girl was dynamite—he had come perilously close to forgetting where he was, and that had never happened to him before. He needed to tread warily and, wrapping his arms around her, he hugged her. 'I knew it would be like this between us.' He stepped back and released her.

Penny gazed bemusedly up at him. She lifted a hand to her full lips. 'You...we...' she stammered. She couldn't say *kissed*, she didn't have the breath. Solo Maffeiano; this incredibly attractive, virile man had kissed her, touched her. It felt more as if she had been hit by lightning. Powerful and sophisticated Solo, and yet she could have sworn she'd heard him groan as well.

'Us, you mean,' Solo amended throatily. 'And there is going to be an us. But not here and not now. The others are waiting for their coffee.' He slipped an arm around her waist to steady her. His eyes, dark as slate, stared down into hers and he saw her shock and confusion and knew she was exactly what he wanted. Innocent, well bred and maternal, she was perfect wife material. To a man who had everything, and had never considered marriage before, the thought of a wife and possibly a child suddenly held strong appeal. 'How old are you, Penelope?' he asked softly.

'Nineteen in September,' she answered without thinking.

'I'm thirty-four, a lot older than you.' And a hell of a lot more experienced, but Solo did not say it. He did not want to frighten her off. She was like a perfect rosebud slowly unfurling. She came alive in his arms, all heat and light and totally unconscious of her potent sensuality.

'Not too old,' she murmured, her fingers curling into his shirt.

He chuckled. 'Good, Penelope, hold that thought, but for the moment coffee.' He ran a soothing hand up and down her spine. Then, cupping her face in his strong hands, he smiled into her eyes and gently kissed the tip of her nose.

'You get the coffee, I'll carry the tray, my hands are steadier than yours are.' And smoothing a few stray tendrils of hair back from her face, he added, 'There—no one will ever guess I have been seducing you in the kitchen.'

'It was only a kiss.' Penny finally managed to speak almost steadily, embarrassed by her headlong capitulation to his overpowering male sexuality.

His slate-grey eyes hardened on her slight, tense frame with a narrow intensity that made her shiver. 'Don't pretend with me, Penelope. The sexual chemistry between us is intense, you know it...accept it, and I promise you won't be disappointed.'

Their eyes met and meshed and something indefinable passed between them.

'Yes,' Penny murmured.

Solo's deep chest heaved and he stepped back a couple of paces. He had her, he thought exultantly. 'I won't rush you, Penelope, except for the coffee!' he added teasingly to lighten the atmosphere.

Walking behind Solo into the dining room, she had to battle to keep down the blush that threatened, convinced the others must know what they had been doing, but no one noticed.

Later she was stunned as they all stood at the front door saying their goodbyes and Solo managed to arrange to come back in two days' time—Saturday—the only time he had free to look over the land, and Penny was to be his guide, because of course her parents and James were going to a house party.

Later, lying in bed going over the events of the evening, she touched her lips and felt again the pressure of Solo's mouth. It had really happened, and she was seeing him on Saturday. She went to sleep with wild dreams of an erotic weekend ahead.

Solo guided the car through the country lanes deep in thought. Once he hit the motorway heading back towards London he turned to Tina. 'Tomorrow send flowers, and an expensive piece of jewellery to Lisa Brunton in New York with a suitable note ending the arrangement. I won't be seeing her again. You know the address.' His decision was made: he was going to marry Penelope Haversham, but first he had to cut all ties with his past liaisons.

'Good idea. I can imagine the dollar signs in her eyes,' Tina agreed.

Saturday morning Penny opened the door to Solo Maffeiano and stared. He was wearing a blue checked shirt, and blue jeans hung low on his hips and moulded his long legs like a second skin. He carried an overnight bag in one hand, and, when she dared to look up into his face, a spasm of sensation clenched her stomach sending her pulse rate flying.

Solo dropped his bag and swept her into his arms. A long kiss later with her head swimming and her legs shaking, he finally set her free.

It was a weekend out of time. Penny introduced him to Mrs Brown, and Brownie insisted on accompanying them when Penny showed him to the room that had been prepared for him.

'I see we really do have a chaperone,' Solo said with a rueful grin when they finally walked out of the house ten minutes later, and got in the car. 'Not that I'm objecting—it is good to know you have been properly looked after.'

She shot him a surprised glance; it seemed an odd thing for him to say. Old-fashioned, but rather honourable, and her happiness ratio went up another notch.

They parked the car at the pub in the village, and walked across the fields. Solo was a fascinating companion. He told her of his travels around the world, and his home in Italy that he managed to go to as often as he could, but not as often as he would like. He made her laugh, and she made him climb over stiles, and hike for miles. But in between they exchanged brief and not so brief kisses, and he continued to tease her sexily until she was unable to think straight.

By the time they sat down to dinner that night, under Brownie's beady eye, Penny knew she was in love for the first time in her life.

Penny leaned over the crib and marvelled at the baby boy. 'He's beautiful—he's going to grow up to be a stunningly handsome man,' she told the doting mother, Patricia, her friend Jane's sister who had arrived from New York the day before. 'Though maybe not as handsome as Solo,' she sighed dreamily. Solo was never out of her thoughts—it had been the most perfect five weeks of her life.

'You are besotted with that man.' Jane laughed. 'You mention his name just about every other sentence.'

'I'm not that bad. Am I?' Penny queried with a grin.

'Do I smell romance in the air, Penny?' Patricia interjected, touching the baby's head. 'He is asleep,' she murmured before sitting down next to Penny on the sofa.

'Maybe.' Penny blushed; she could not help it.

'And you should see him, Patricia,' Jane cut in. 'Tall, dark and handsome does not cover it, add rich and he is every girl's dream.'

Patricia gave Penny a searching look. 'He sounds too good to be true. I hope you're being careful,' she went on bluntly. 'You don't want to end up another statistic in the unmarried mothers list.'

Chance would be a fine thing, Penny thought wistfully. Solo had taken her out every weekend, and she had just about offered herself on a plate. But he had a lot more self-control than she did. He always called a halt before they went too far. She admired him for his strong principle, but it did not stop her aching in bed every night.

'He is not like that,' Penny defended. 'He respects me.'

'My, my,' Patricia drawled teasingly. 'The boy must be a paragon of virtue, if he does not want to get into your knickers.'

'Please.' Penny blushed scarlet again. 'It is not like that.'

'Unless of course he is a virgin like yourself,' Patricia offered with a grin.

Jane spluttered, 'He is no boy, and I'd bet my life savings he is no virgin,' and went off into paroxysms of laughter.

Penny had never thought of Solo with another woman, but Jane's words forced her to. Solo was a healthy, virile male, a lot older than she was; he was bound to have dated, even loved other women, and it hurt.

'Do you mind?' Penny snapped. 'It is not a joke. Solo is the man I am going to marry.'

'What?' Jane exclaimed, her laughter vanishing. 'The hunk has actually asked you?'

'Well, almost,' Penny amended, and did what she had been dying to do all week—she confided her secret hope to Jane and Patricia. 'When Solo came down last Saturday, he had a talk with my father, but then his PA called him and he had to leave suddenly. But when I saw Solo out to his car, he said he had something very important to ask me when he got back. Plus all week my father has been grinning at me, as if he knows something I don't.' The relief at being able to share her excitement with her friends was heady. 'Solo telephoned me yesterday. He is coming back tomorrow, and he has planned a special dinner in London for the two of us. What else could it all mean?' she asked, turning sparkling eyes on her friends.

'If you are right, this is serious,' Patricia said bluntly. 'You're only eighteen.'

'I'm nineteen next week,' Penny said swiftly.

'Even so, I thought you were going to Cambridge University with Jane.'

Shamefaced, Penny turned to Jane. 'I know we are booked into the halls of residence together for the first year, but I really do love him.' Then as another thought occurred to her a smile lightened her eyes, and she added, 'Though maybe I can still go to university. Solo has his work, and he has to go abroad a lot. We haven't discussed it, but we could probably live between here and Cambridge.'

'Wait a minute.' Patricia adopted her older-sister mode, hands on hips. 'What's his name? Where did you meet him? And what exactly does he do?'

'His name is Solo Maffeiano, he is an Italian businessman and he is gorgeous,' Penny began enthusiastically. 'And I met him when Daddy invited him down on business. Daddy has sold him some of the farmland to develop, I think.' But business was not Penny's interest, Solo was, and she lifted her head, smiling, but was stunned by the look of horror on Patricia's face.

'Solo Maffeiano. *The* Solo Maffeiano?'

'That's his name,' Penny said cautiously, a sense of unease curling her stomach. 'Why, do you know him?'

'I've met him once in New York. He's tall, dark and very handsome but I know a lot about him. He dated Lisa, a partner in my husband's law firm, for months. Lisa was madly in love with him and she thought he would marry her, so she was heartbroken when he finished with her four weeks ago.'

'It can't be the same man,' Penny said stoutly. She had known him five weeks!

'There could not be two Solo Maffeianos in the world. His financial acumen and his prowess with woman are legend.'

'Yes, there could.' Penny clung onto the hope.

'Penny, the man is in the same line of business.'

'Well, even if it is the same man, maybe he realised he didn't truly love your friend. That is not his fault,' she said, trying to defend Solo.

'If that was all, maybe not,' Patricia said soberly. 'But when Lisa received a goodbye gift of roses and a diamond pin, she called him and discovered he had not even sent them but his PA. Tina Jenson. How low is that?'

Penny felt her heart shrivel in her chest at the mention of Tina Jenson. Patricia was right—it had to be the same Solo. 'Maybe he didn't have time,' she said faintly, but she was clutching at straws and she knew it.

'Oh, you poor kid, Penny. What have you got into? According to Lisa, Solo Maffeiano is a ruthless, powerful man. Nobody knows much about his early years, just that he had made his first million by the time he was twenty-two, and nobody asks too closely how! In fact, rumour has it Tina, his American PA, is his permanent lover. The only reason they are not married is she has a husband tucked away somewhere who won't divorce her.'

Penny felt the blood drain from her face. 'No. I don't believe it.'

'Penny, you're young,' Patricia said gently 'Maybe you're right and Solo Maffeiano is totally genuine in his feelings for you, but the man is too old for you. Give yourself time. Don't be rushed into marriage. You said Solo has bought some of your father's land. How do you know he is not after the house and park as well?'

'No…I don't know, but he is not too old for me.' she ended defiantly, wishing she had never come to visit Jane today and never heard Patricia's denouncement of Solo.

'Do me a favour, Penny. If Maffeiano does ask you to marry him, take your time before making a decision. You are an intelligent girl, with your whole future before you, a pedigree a mile long, and you stand to inherit a very desirable property.'

'Rubbish, nobody cares about things like that any more,' Penny exploded.

'Your stepmother Veronica does, and I think a man like Solo Maffeiano does as well. Promise me, before you do anything drastic you will at least start at university.'

'I'll think about it,' Penny murmured in a very subdued voice.

'If the man loves you, Penny, he won't mind.'

'Who loves our little Penny?' Simon burst into the room. 'Besides me,' he teased. Tall, tanned with blond hair, he grinned at the three women.

'Oh, shut up, Simon and get out,' Jane snapped.

Penny got to her feet. 'No.' She glanced at Simon. 'Stay. I have to go.'

'I'll see you out.' Jane jumped up, and, once in the hall of the vicarage, Jane put an arm around Penny's shoulder. 'Don't worry about university or me. Talk to Solo—I'm sure it will be fine. You know Patricia, she always was a terrible gossip. You don't have to believe everything she tells you.'

The sun was shining, it was a beautiful warm September afternoon, but to Penny the world had turned grey as she set off walking through the village, a deep frown marring her lovely features. She needed to think, and, turning, she trekked across the fields towards home.

Solo with another woman. She examined the thought and she didn't like it. He had finished with the woman within a week of meeting Penny, which she could just about get over. But what Patricia had said about Tina Jenson she could not dismiss quite so easily. Penny had only met the woman once, and she had taken Tina's position as Solo's PA at face value.

Solo had hinted to Penny he wanted to marry her, and she would stake her life on him being sincere. She loved him with all her heart. Was she really going to let Patricia's vague rumours and gossip spoil the love and trust she had in Solo?

No, she finally decided with the optimism of youth. Tomorrow Solo would be here and everything would be fine, and, holding that thought, she hurried on home.

Penny saw the black car as soon as she walked around the corner of the house. It was Solo's—he had come back early, and her confidence in his love rose sky high. She heard voices as she passed the open window of the drawing room, and paused. But it was the 'Solo, darling really!' that stopped her in her tracks.

She leant against the warm stone wall beneath the window, unable to move, and for once grateful for her lack of height. She had only heard the voice once before but it was unmistakably Tina Jenson.

'I have seen the amount of money you have paid for the land, and it's not worth it on its own. What are you up to?'

'It s a good long-term investment, and I'm thinking of going into a partnership,' Solo responded smoothly.

'I don't believe you. You always work alone.' Tina paused, then added, 'But then it's not like you to buy a lump of land. With the house and park, yes, I could understand. The building is historic, and with work could be turned into a luxury hotel. But even so the place is shabby, and it would cost a fortune to renovate. No, I have known you too long…You are up to something, Solo.' She ended with a chuckle.

Penny's spine stiffened, her pride in her home coming to the fore, and she waited for Solo to deny Tina's words.

'You obviously don't know me that well,' Solo opined, 'or you would know I have every intention of refurbishing this place and going into a partnership, but not necessarily with

Julian Haversham. You seem to have over-
looked the delightful Penelope, and it is about
time I settled down.'

'What? Seduce the daughter? That child.'
Tina laughed out loud. 'So she will go along
with your plan for the house!'

Numb with shock and totally humiliated,
Penny sank to her knees on the hard ground.
She wanted to put her hands over her ears but
a masochistic desire to know the worst made
her hold back her cry of despair, and she made
herself listen.

'Come off it, Solo, you can be ruthless in
business, but you're not the type to seduce a
young girl. Penny Haversham is lovely, but
she is the kind a man has to marry, and I can't
see you doing that. Solo by name, Solo by nature. You like your women to know the score.
Sex without commitment. I should know. I
have sent the flowers and picked out the jewellery often enough.'

'True, but only because you are much more
sensitive to a woman's needs in that area,'
Solo drawled with mocking amusement. 'But
maybe I've reached an age when I want some-

thing different. A loving wife and a son or two holds strong appeal.'

'Oh, sure, a malleable little wife while you do what you like. I can see the appeal, but I hate to tell you, Solo, young girls have a nasty habit of growing up, and Penelope Haversham is no fool; unworldly, yes, but to get a place at Cambridge University she has to have a brain,' she said cynically. 'And have you thought of how you would explain our relationship to a wife? She would need to be enormously broad-minded,' she ended with a laugh.

'Nothing would change between you and I,' Solo said with a responsive chuckle. 'You don't need to worry on that score. I'll always love you…'

Patricia had been right, and, sick to her soul, Penny did not stop to hear more, but scuttled back around the corner of the house. Her eyes swimming in tears, blindly she ran and ran back over the fields and finally collapsed in her secret place, beneath a huge willow by the river.

Fighting to breathe, her body racked with gigantic shudders. She cried until there were no tears left. Her throat was sore and aching, but was nothing like the ache in her heart. Still the words of Solo and Tina, their shared laughter, echoed in her head like some horrific nightmare that would not go away. Her dreams of love and marriage completely shattered—it had just been an illusion created by the deceit of one man.

Solo had considered marrying her; in that she had been right. But he did not want her, did not love her, never had. It had all been a sophisticated game, a plan to acquire her acceptance for the changes in store at Haversham Park, and as the knowledge sank into her tortured mind she heard her heart break.

Penny slipped from her hiding place and stared at the softly flowing water, and wanted to die; she could not bear the pain. Lifting her head, she looked up at the clear blue sky, the only sound an occasional bird song and the gentle flow of the water over the stones. But as she stood there with the water swirling around her the familiar beauty of the place touched her soul, and she realised life was too precious to let a womanising devil of a man like Solo Maffeiano destroy her.

Slowly Penny walked back across the fields towards the vicarage. She couldn't go home yet... She could not face Solo.

She needed to build up her courage to dump the swine, and face her father. She could not bear the thought of him actually going into business with Maffeiano, and selling the house even though he had every right to do so, and if her rejection of Solo spoilt her dad's plans, tough... But she could see Veronica's hand behind this.

Penny consoled herself with the thought that at least her father had got the money for the land. He and Veronica would have to be happy with that. She was almost at the front door of the vicarage when it flew open and Simon appeared.

'What the hell happened to you?' he demanded. 'You look as though you have been dragged through a hedge backwards.'

Penny looked up into his friendly face and she could not help it, she threw herself into his arms. 'Oh, Simon, Patricia was right about the man I thought loved me—he doesn't at all. I am in a hell of a mess, and I dare not face Solo Maffeiano.'

'Hey, don't be upset. Your honorary brother is here to help.' His strong arms closed firmly around her, and he tilted her chin up to his. 'Jane told me you were involved with a man.'

'Not any more—I never want to see him again,' Penny said bitterly.

'This Solo wouldn't be a tall, dark, good-looking dude...?

'Yes, why?'

'He's walking up the drive, probably looking for you. Follow my lead and your troubles will be over. He looks the jealous type. Kiss me and make it look good. Then tell him you were waiting for me, your boyfriend.' Simon pressed his lips to hers and Penny wrapped her arms around his neck and clung to him...

CHAPTER ONE

'I REALLY don't feel like socialising, Jane.' Penny made one last effort to get out of accompanying Jane to her firm's dinner-dance as they got out of the taxi outside an exclusive London hotel.

'Yes, you do.' Jane grabbed Penny's arm and almost frogmarched her into the impressive entrance foyer. 'After the shock you have had today you need company. Relax, forget your worries and act your age for once, instead of like an old spinster.'

'But I feel half naked in this dress.' Jane had insisted on lending her the dress, when Penny had tried to use the excuse of having nothing with her to wear. 'I never wear red,' Penny wailed as they handed their wraps in to the cloakroom attendant.

'You look great. Stop moaning and enjoy yourself.'

*   *   *

Solo Maffeiano walked out of the lounge bar and stilled, tension in every long line of his superb body. He looked and looked again at the lady in red. His grey eyes flared in shock: it was Penelope Haversham in person. But not a side of Miss Haversham he had ever seen before...which was hardly surprising as she had played the young innocent for him. It still rankled that she had managed to fool him.

But there was no mistaking the delicate profile. Her pale hair was swept up into an intricate twist on the top of her head. Her translucent skin. Though tonight there was a lot of bare skin, he thought with a cynical twist of his hard mouth. The slight coltishness of youth had gone and she had grown into a strikingly sensual woman. The shimmering red dress clung to her every curve; it was cut low at the front and even lower at the back. With her high, full breasts, a tiny waist and firmly rounded bottom, she had the perfect hourglass figure. Add shapely legs and the fact that she moved like a dream oozing sex appeal, and she became every red-blooded male's fantasy female. Nothing like the demure bridesmaid in the photograph Solo had first noted.

But what was she doing in his hotel? Had she come looking for him? Perhaps she thought she could seduce him into doing what she wanted more easily in the intimate surroundings of his suite, rather than waiting until their official appointment tomorrow. The thought was seductive, and she was certainly dressed for the part.

Then he spotted her friend Jane and the direction they were heading. He realised it was pure coincidence after all as the two women were swept up in a crowd entering the ballroom, and he felt the sudden jolt of desire again.

Damn it to hell! She still had the same effect on him. Even though he knew her for the two-timing, scheming little bitch she was. Red was a very appropriate colour for her type. His grey eyes narrowed menacingly, the anger was buried deep, but it was still there...

For a moment he was tempted to follow Penny and make his presence felt, but cynically decided not to. It would be interesting to

see which Penny would appear in his office tomorrow—the-butter-wouldn't-melt-in-her-mouth
Penny, or the sexy lady-in-red Penny.

Four years later he still smarted from the
blow to his pride Penelope Haversham had in-
flicted. Since the age of twelve, no woman had
ever turned Solo Maffeiano down, and no
woman had deceived him so thoroughly then
dumped him. No other woman had even tried,
only Penelope, and she had succeeded.

His memory of their brief, disastrous affair
four years earlier still had the power to make
his blood boil. It had not even been an affair,
because being an idiot he had never taken her
to bed. For the first time in his life he had
decided to commit to one woman for life and
got stamped on for his pains. This time would
be different, he vowed with a chilling smile
that never reached steel-grey eyes. He spun on
his heel and re-entered the bar. He had not
expected to see her here tonight, and he needed
a drink.

Enjoy herself? If only she could, Penny
thought, a prickling sensation bringing her out

in goose-bumps. Convinced someone was watching her, she glanced swiftly around and felt a fool. Her nerves must be getting the better of her—it was only a dinner-dance. Get a grip, she told herself as they walked into the ballroom.

As for fun, there had been very little in Penny's life recently. Her father and Veronica had been involved in a rail crash nine months ago. Veronica had died instantly, and her father two days later without ever regaining consciousness, and it had changed Penny's life.

She had graduated from university last year with Jane. Jane had got a job in the legal department of a finance company, and rented a tiny two-bedroom terraced house in London. Penny had planned on joining her, having secured a job in the British Library, but the accident that had killed Julian and Veronica had also killed her plan to live in London.

Instead Penny had stayed at home to look after her brother James, and grieved, while still having to deal with all the details of two deaths and the ongoing accident investigation.

Today Penny had come up to London on business and to stay with Jane for two days. Jane's family was looking after James.

In a buoyant mood, Penny had actually thought she was beginning to get over the worst of her grief and feel hope for the future. It had been a perfect May morning when she had set off for her meeting with her publishing house, and to her delight she had signed a contract for four more children's books. The first was already at the printers'.

It had been James who had given her the idea. By the age of three he had already learnt to read simple books, and when Penny was at home he loved her telling him bedtime tales, that were often based on historical fact. She had looked for some early learning books on history and been unable to find any.

So she had written and illustrated one. James had loved it, and after her final exams were over last June, she had sent it to a publishing house. With the death of her father and Veronica, she had forgotten all about it, until she had received a letter saying they liked it and were going to publish it and suggested she wrote a whole series.

In the afternoon she had had an appointment with Mr Simpson, her father's lawyer. Thinking the will had passed probate, she had walked into his office, happier than she had been in months, and hoping for more good news.

Mr Simpson had gone over the will again. He had informed her Mrs Brown's pension was secure and there was a reasonable amount of cash divided between Penny and James equally, and in the event of Veronica's death Penny would be James's legal guardian. Penny had been aware of all this, and she'd already known Haversham Park was hers, because he had read the will out after the funeral.

'Now we come to the hard part, so to speak,' Mr Simpson said gruffly. 'Your father was a lovely man, but paperwork was not his forte. Another document has come to light, perfectly legal and above board, but the actuality is you only inherit a half-share in Haversham Park. It seems your father sold the other half to a third party.'

The news came as a complete body-blow to Penny. She could not believe it. 'What?' she exclaimed, her eyes widening in horror. 'A third party, I don't believe it! Daddy would have told me.' Someone else owned half her home! The thought was mind-boggling. What was she supposed to do—share her home, or split the house down the middle? She had the hysterical desire to laugh—the whole idea was ludicrous. But one look at Mr Simpson's serious face and she knew he was not joking.

Penny paled as a premonition that worse was to come filled her mind. She had to ask the question, but her mouth was suddenly dry.

'I don't know why he didn't,' Mr Simpson continued. 'But I have to tell you the inheritance tax on the value of your father's estate is quite considerable.' He mentioned a figure that had her mouth falling open in shock. 'If you don't sell your share of Haversham Park you can't pay the inheritance tax and you will eventually be declared bankrupt, and the house will be sold anyway by the Inland Revenue.' Things could not get worse, but they did…

'But it is not all bad. I have spoken to the other party.'

'Who is the other party?' Penny asked hoarsely, finally managing to speak.

'Well, that is the good news. He is an Italian gentleman, a Mr Solo Maffeiano.'

At the mention of Solo, the little colour left in Penny's face drained away, her stomach heaved. Solo Maffeiano owned half her home. No, no, no, she screamed silently. Life could not be so cruel. But as Mr Simpson's voice droned on she was forced to accept it could.

'He tells me you know each other, and he is quite agreeable to talk over the options available. You sell to him or you put the place on the open market and share the proceeds. Either way, Penelope, you will be all right.' Mr Simpson actually smiled.

Penny shivered, nausea clawing at her stomach, and she could not respond.

'You can buy a smaller place, much more sensible for you and James. The inheritance tax can be paid, and you will still have enough to live on plus the money to set up a trust fund for your brother's education.' Mr Simpson beamed and looked at Penny and he realised his client was far from happy. She looked terrified, as though the weight of the world had just fallen on her shoulders.

He stood up from behind his desk and walked around to Penny, putting a fatherly hand on her drooping shoulder. 'I realise it has come as a shock to you, my dear. But, believe me, selling is the sensible solution, the only solution.'

Penny shook her head, and dragged herself up on shaking legs. 'There must be something I can do,' she pleaded, 'Rather than involve Mr Maff…eiano.' She choked on his name. To have to sell her home was horrific, but not half as bad as the thought she might have to see Solo again. He had hurt her so much in the past she couldn't bear to face him. 'If I must sell the house, please, you arrange it for me, Mr Simpson.'

'Don't worry, Penelope, it is all in hand. I have taken the liberty of setting up a meeting for you tomorrow at noon at Maffeiano's London office.'

'Please could you go for me? Whatever you arrange I'll accept, but keep me out of it.'

'I'm afraid I can't do that. Mr Maffeiano has insisted on dealing with you personally. But it will work out fine, I'm sure.' Mr Simpson pressed a card with the address on it into her hand. 'Now, why don't you run along and do some shopping, cheer yourself up?'

Mr Simpson looked pleased, while Penny looked sick when she had finally left the lawyer's office. She could not believe what had happened; it was her worst nightmare realised. She was dreading having to meet Solo again, but she had no choice.

She could vividly remember the horrendous scene when Solo had caught her in the arms of Simon. Incredulous anger had been followed by a tirade of what had sounded like curses in Italian and then, as if a switch had been thrown in his brain, he'd stepped back, coldly remote and in complete control.

Acting for all she was worth, Penny had told Solo she was sorry if she had given him the wrong impression, but Simon had always been

her boyfriend, and she had only dated Solo because Simon had been away.

Even now she still shivered when she remembered the look of icy contempt Solo had
slashed at her, before in the next moment
Simon had played his part.

'Penny and I have been a couple for ages,
and I know her well. When her stepmother
asked her to be nice to you she was too soft-
hearted to say no—she doesn't like to hurt
people. You do understand, sir,' and the *sir*
had simply accentuated the age difference.

'Yes, I understand perfectly,' Solo had
drawled. His handsome face devoid of all expression, and his grey eyes cold and hard as
the Arctic waste, had frozen her to the spot.
'Congratulations, Penny, I do believe Veronica
has finally met her match.' And swinging on
his heel, he had stalked off.

After the fatal day when she had lied to Solo
and he had left, life had never been quite the
same at Haversham Park. Her father had told
her Solo had called but had had to leave in a
hurry. Her father had continued saying he was

sure Solo would be in touch as he was very fond of her.

Penny had responded, lying through her teeth, 'Maybe, but he is far too old for me, and I'm going to university with Jane. We are really looking forward to meeting other young people, laying the groundwork for a good career.'

Her father had looked shocked, and then worried, before sighing and saying, 'You're very young; I should have expected it.'

Three weeks later when Penny had left for university and there had been no contact with Solo, Veronica had realised something was wrong, and accused Penny of destroying the best chance her father had ever had of making a fortune.

'It was obvious Solo fancied you. You should have given him more encouragement. What girl needs an education when they can hook a millionaire like Solo Maffeiano? You're an idiot.' Which had summed up Veronica's slant on life, Penny had thought dryly.

'For heaven's sake, cheer up, woman,' Jane's voice cut into her troubled thoughts. 'Sell the mouldering old pile and get a life like me.'

For the next couple of hours Penny did try. But the thought of the meeting tomorrow prevented Penny relaxing and she was glad when the evening was finally over and they returned to Jane's house.

At five minutes to noon Penny walked into the building that housed the London offices of the Maffeiano Corporation. She glanced across the marble-floored foyer to where a smart brunette sat at a long, curved desk, bearing the word 'Reception' on a gold plaque.

Taking a deep breath, Penny pulled the jacket of her black suit down to her hips and walked to the desk. 'Excuse me, I have an appointment with Mr Maffeiano.'

The receptionist's gaze slid over Penny's slender figure dressed in the neat black suit, with the white blouse beneath, the blonde hair scraped back in a bun, and the pale face. '*You* have an appointment with Mr Maffeiano?'

Bristling, Penny affirmed with a nod, 'Yes.' So she didn't look like his usual model woman, so what! At college she'd had no trouble fighting off a succession of young men more interested in her looks than her brain. Then during nine months as a mother to James she had developed a firm belief in her own intellectual talents, and ability to cope with any eventuality. This was business, strictly business, and she could handle it.

'I'll call his secretary. Take a seat.' The girl gestured to a seating arrangement surrounding a table holding magazines.

Penny was glad to sit down because her legs were suddenly weak. If the girl did but know Penny did not want to be here, only the decision had been taken out of her hands. She had not slept a wink last night, the enormity of what had happened was almost destroying her.

Over and over again she asked herself why her father would have done such thing, but could not find an answer. The only certainty was that she had lost the family home. The only decision left was where the house would go—to Solo or to a stranger—and that was not up to her, but to Solo. She dreaded the prospect of meeting him again.

'Miss Haversham.' A grey-haired lady in her fifties approached Penny. 'Will you come this way, please?'

'Thank you.' Penny tried a smile and followed the lady down a long, carpeted corridor.

The secretary opened a door at the end, and gestured Penny to enter before her. 'You can wait here. Mr Maffeiano is delayed, but he won't be long. Help yourself to coffee,' she said, indicating a coffeemaker that stood on a small table in one corner of what was obviously an office. The woman took a seat behind a large computer desk. 'You look as though you need a fix, my dear,' and she smiled, suddenly looking very human.

'No... No, thank you.' Penny returned the smile, her head turning when a double door that she surmised led to the inner sanctum was opened and a woman walked out. Penny stifled a silent groan. Tina Jenson...

'Hello—well, if it isn't little Penny Haversham,' the tall redhead drawled, then added, 'I'm surprised you have the nerve to face Solo after the stroke you pulled.'

'And hello to you too.' Penny said dryly. Why should she be surprised to see Tina? The woman was Solo's Personal Assistant and long-time lover. If any stroke had been pulled, it had been by Solo Maffeiano on her father, she thought angrily. Her father had been no businessman, Penny would be the first to admit. Solo had to have tricked him, anything else she could not contemplate. She had adored her dad; still did, she thought sadly.

'You have nerve, I'll give you that,' Tina said shortly, and, with a goodbye to the secretary, swept out of the office.

Penny watched her leave with mixed feelings. It was only the second time she had met the woman, but Tina did not improve on acquaintance, she thought bitterly. Obviously Tina and Solo were still together, and Penny refused to believe the slight pain in her heart was anything other than a touch of heartburn. She had not eaten anything since yesterday.

Penny glanced at the coffee but dismissed the idea, and sat down on one of the chairs provided. All she'd had for breakfast were three cups of black coffee, and she was nervous and angry enough without having another shot of caffeine. She clasped her hands around her purse in her lap in a deathlike grip and waited.

'He will see you now,' the secretary announced as a green light on the console flashed, and, indicating the door to Penny, she added, 'But please make it quick, he does not have much time. His meeting with Mrs Jenson took longer than expected.'

I'll just bet it did! Penny thought unkindly. A kiss and a cuddle, or maybe more had delayed him! Rising to her feet, Penny straightened her shoulders and with a brief, 'Thank you,' in the secretary's direction she walked into Solo's office.

Warily she glanced around the elegant room. Dark panelling, a polished wood floor with what looked like a very expensive carpet, a black leather sofa and chair, and by the massive window that filled almost a whole wall was an enormous mahogany desk and a high-backed chair. But no Solo Maffeiano!

She walked slowly into the room, her heart racing. It was hot. May and the central heating was still on. Not a luxury Penny could afford at Haversham Park, she thought wryly. She unfastened the jacket of her suit, and pulled at the collar of her blouse.

Maybe it was deliberate. Solo Maffeiano was the sort who would like to make a client sweat, she thought bitterly, taking a deep breath and slowly exhaling before she forced her feet onwards to the desk. She stopped at the edge, at a loss as to what to do next. She tried a polite cough, her throat tightening in the process.

Slowly the chair swung around and she saw Solo and her breath stuck in her throat. Their eyes met and she almost passed out. It was the fiercest electric connection she had ever experienced in her life. She blinked, and when she looked again, like a replay of her eighteen-year-old self, she was totally intoxicated by the sheer animal magnetism of the man that the years in between had done nothing to dispel.

To disconcert her even more Solo was lounging back in the chair, his jacket and tie discarded, the tailored white shirt fitting his broad shoulders to perfection, the collar open at the neck to reveal the strong, tanned throat and a glimpse of black chest hair. Her pulse raced, and her mouth went dry; she could not have spoken to save her life.

'The honourable Penelope Haversham,' he drawled sarcastically. 'Allow me.' He rose to his feet and walked around the desk.

She watched him move, six feet three of stunningly attractive male. She had forgotten quite how tall Solo was, and how he projected a power, a raw sexuality that made her stomach muscles clench in helpless response. From the top of his dark head, to the broad shoulders, to the dark pleated trousers that settled on his lean hips and long legs, he was the epitome of predatory male and she could not help staring.

Her fascinated gaze watched as he took a chair from against the wall and placed it beside her. Realising she was staring, Penny jerked back her head and felt a painful tide of red wash over her face. She was ogling the man like an idiot.

'Sit down,' Solo commanded coldly.

She was glad to oblige, as her legs were shaking. 'Thank you, Mr Maffeiano,' she murmured politely, and was aware of him resuming his seat at the opposite side of the desk.

'Mr Maffeiano,' he drawled mockingly. Ice-grey eyes cut like a laser into hers, then slowly swept over her slender body with a frigid disdain that even now, after so many years had the power to make her cringe. It was the exact same look he had given her when he had caught her kissing Simon, as though she was beneath contempt.

'Surely you and I are on first-name terms at least, Penny?'

She blushed even redder. 'Yes, of course, Solo,' she muttered, her tongue sticking to the roof of her dry mouth.

She was behaving like a fool. She was no longer a naive young girl, with a head full of romantic ideals of love and marriage, an easy conquest for a ruthless, sophisticated man of the world like Solo. She should be thanking her lucky stars that she had seen through the devil in time, instead of sitting here, trembling and blushing like a schoolgirl.

'Well, let's get down to business—I haven't much time to spare.' His deep voice was curt. 'I have a luncheon engagement at one.'

Warily she watched him as he shoved his chair back a little, and flung one arm casually over the back. Nervously she straightened the hem of her skirt over her knees.

His grey eyes followed the movement of her hands and narrowed to linger on her legs, and the charged sexuality of the knowing look he swept slowly over her body made heat surge in her face, and, to her shame, another more intimate place. The shockingly helpless flare of response made her press her knees together, her body became taut, and she wanted to curl up and hide.

His expressive mouth twisted in a cynical smile. 'Still as demure as ever, I see.' Solo had a vivid image of the lady in red last night and wanted to laugh out loud at the image Penny presented today in the black suit, the conservative court shoes, and the hair scraped back.

Who did she think she was fooling? Certainly not him...

Appalled at her own weakness, Penny murmured, 'Yes,' as she stiffened her shoulders, not knowing what else to say. Simply being in the same room with Solo again had a disastrous effect on her mental powers. One look at him and every sensible thought vanished from her head, and she knew she needed all her wits about her to discuss business with the man.

He had been thirty-four when she'd first met him, and well aware of his impact on the female of the species. Suave and devastatingly attractive, he could charm the birds right out of the trees. His deep, melodious voice tinged with a hint of sensuality had promised untold delight, with perhaps just a touch of danger. Now as she looked up into his cold eyes all she saw was danger...

Almost four years had left their mark. His curly hair was ruthlessly swept back from his broad brow. There was harshness about the firmly chiselled features, a ruthlessness in the grey eyes that met her own that said he was a man in firm control of himself and all those around him. A man to be respected for his immense power and wealth, but also a man to be feared.

'If you say so.' His gaze moved with leisurely insolence over her face, and lower to the firm swell of her breasts against the soft cotton of her blouse. 'It has been a long time but you haven't changed at all, Penelope.'

Penny's body responded with another sudden rush of heat that horrified her. Slender fingers curled into fists, her nails digging into her palms until it hurt, trying to distract her traitorous body with pain. What a choice! she thought dryly, and the sheer stupidity of injuring herself enabled her to relax her grip.

'Neither have you, Solo,' she said stiffly, hoping she sounded sophisticated and, praying her voice would not wobble, she added, 'And I'll take that as a compliment.'

'Take it any way you like,' he drawled. 'But back to business. What exactly do you want?' One dark brow arched enquiringly.

'Well. I...you... Mr Simpson said...' she stammered to a halt.

Solo rose slowly to his feet and in a few lithe strides was around the desk and towering over her. 'You seem a little nervous. Shall we start again? After all, we were close friends once.' Holding out his hand, he added, 'Good to see you, Penny.'

Penny looked at his hand as if it were a snake that might bite. She glanced up into his eyes and saw the mocking amusement in their silvery depths. The swine was laughing at her.

'Yes, of course.' she said firmly and placed her hand in his. His hand squeezed hers, sending a prickling sensation scooting up her arm.

Instinctively Penny tensed, and lowered her eyes from his knowing gaze. Her head was telling her to get out of there as quickly as possible, while her traitorous heart skipped a beat as the hand that gripped hers tightened fractionally, before he set her free.

Solo looked at her lowered head. 'You have changed, after all,' he drawled mockingly. 'At one time you were not afraid to face me.'

Pride alone made her tip back her head and look up. 'I'm not now,' she denied curtly. 'I'm just surprised you wanted to see me, instead of

Mr Simpson, my lawyer, after the way we parted,' she said with blunt honesty.

'Some you win, some you lose.' One shoulder elevated in a shrug.

Penny's eyes widened in surprise on his dark, inscrutable face. He was as good as admitting it had all been a game to him four years ago, and she, poor fool that she was, had felt guilty over the blunt way she had dismissed him. The anger that had been simmering inside her ever since Mr Simpson had told her the news yesterday came bubbling to the surface.

'But you never lose, do you, Solo?' she said hotly. 'What I want to know is how the hell you conned my father into selling you half of Haversham Park.'

His silver-grey eyes hardened perceptibly, his handsome face an expressionless mask. 'Be very careful of throwing unfounded accusations around. I allow no one to cast a slur on my integrity without taking legal action, and, given the mess you are in at the moment, bankruptcy would be the result.'

'I'm not far from it anyway,' she snapped back bitterly, recalling the inheritance tax, and it was enough to make her clamp down on her anger. Insulting the man was not going to help her situation. She needed Solo's agreement, either to buy her out or to sell the house to someone else.

She had overreacted. Shock at seeing him had churned up emotions she had thought she had successfully buried. Solo Maffeiano might still have the charisma, the blatant sexuality that had the power to awaken old familiar feelings inside her. But she was older and wiser now, and knew it wasn't love, just lust, and easily denied. She only had to remember the way he had tried to manipulate her feelings for the sake of the house.

A wry smile tugged her mouth, the irony of the situation hitting her. With her late father's help it looked as if Solo would get the house anyway. But at least she was not stuck with a man who had quite happily toyed with her foolish heart, while betraying her with the elegant Tina Jenson.

The fact that Tina Jenson was still with him simply confirmed Solo's guilt in Penny's eyes. He was a ruthless, devious bastard, and she had had a lucky escape.

'That is a very secretive smile,' Solo prompted. 'Care to share the joke?'

'It was nothing,' Penny said, and in that moment she realised Solo was nothing to her, and she smiled with genuine relief.

'I don't want to waste any more of your valuable time. My lawyer informs me you own half my home. How, he wasn't quite clear.' She could not resist the dig and cast a swift glance up at him beneath the thick fringe of her lashes. She still did not understand why her father would have done such a thing, but he had, and she had to deal with the consequences.

'Strictly legitimate, I can assure you,' Solo informed her coldly.

'Yes, so I understand, and that is why I am here.' She lowered her eyes. 'I want you to buy me out or agree to put the house on the open market,' Penny stated simply.

She knew Solo had not developed the land he had bought from her father, apparently losing interest in the project. When Veronica was alive she had never stopped telling Penny that it was all her fault.

Penny had had no answer to her stepmother's accusations—well, none she'd wanted to tell her—and instead Penny had suffered in silence. While Solo Maffeiano had vanished from their lives and, as far as she knew, the acreage he had bought was rented out to adjoining farmers.

'My, my, you actually want to sell your home?' His sarcastic tone cut into her musings, and she glanced back up into his dark, sardonic face. 'And I have first refusal.' A slow smile twisted his hard mouth and chilled her to the bone. 'What an interesting scenario, and surprising. I seem to remember you were very attached to the ancestral pile. What has changed?'

'Apparently you own half,' she said scathingly. 'And I wouldn't share so much as a minute with you, given a choice. Therefore I have no alternative. The inheritance tax has to be paid, and I don't have the money.' He knew all this; he was just trying to make her squirm. 'But you know all this. Mr Simpson spoke to you.'

'I do, but I wanted to hear it from your own sweet lips,' Solo said with cold derision.

Penny studied his hard face with bitter eyes. What he really meant was he wanted to humiliate her. Because she had had the temerity to dump him, and he was not averse to a little revenge. 'Yes, well, you have now, so can I have your answer?' she snapped back.

'No. I'll need to think about it, and it will take me rather more than a *minute*,' he drawled sarcastically. 'In the meantime you can tell me what you have been doing the last few years.'

He was supposed to be in a hurry—it didn't sound like it, Penny thought, simmering with resentment. And she wished he would go and sit down. He was too close and towering over her like some dark avenging angel. It was giving her a crick in the neck simply to look at him, and, fixing her gaze to a spot on his left shoulder, she began a catalogue of her life to date.

'I went to university for three years, got my degree. Then I secured a job at the British Library to start last September. I was going to share a house with Jane. But I never got the chance because Daddy and Veronica were killed in a rail crash. They had spent the summer in France as usual, and ironically the crash was when they were nearly home, only a few miles outside of London. So now of course I look after my brother full-time.' She saw no reason to tell him about her new career as a writer of educational books for children. The less he knew about her, the better.

'So where is James now?' Solo queried lightly.

'Jane's parents, the Reverend Turner and his wife, with their older daughter Patricia who is visiting from America with her son, kindly offered to take him with them on holiday. It is the first time we have been apart since our loss.'

She did not add that the vicar and his wife, who were like honorary grandparents to James, had had to talk her into it. Mrs Turner ran the playgroup James attended and he knew them very well. Penny had only agreed after Mrs Turner had pointed out James would enjoy the holiday, plus Patricia's son would be there for him to play with. Nor did she notice the gleam of satisfaction in Solo's cold eyes as he turned his back to her.

'I was sorry to hear of your parents' death. I was in South America at the time and could not attend the funeral.' Solo straightened something on his desk and turned and leant against it.

Watching him leaning negligently against the desk, with a bit of space between them, Penny could almost convince herself this was a normal conversation.

'Thank you for the wreath,' she said quietly, remembering how surprised she had been at the funeral to discover Solo Maffeiano had sent flowers. Because after she had split up with him, as far as she knew, her dad and Veronica had never seen him again.

'My pleasure, your father was a decent man.'

He was to you! she wanted to snipe. Because even after seeing it in black and white she still had difficulty believing her father would have sold him half the house without telling Penny. But antagonising Solo would get her nowhere. Be civil, and get out as quick as you can, she told herself, so instead she agreed.

'Yes, he was, and I still miss him. But James and I are pulling through, and of course Brownie is an enormous help.'

'And what happened to the blond-haired Adonis?' He slanted a glance at her ringless fingers. 'Simon, wasn't it?' The question was asked so casually Penny answered without thinking.

'The last Jane heard he was in Africa teaching English.' She smiled fondly, thinking of Simon. 'But Simon is not much of a letter writer, he could just as easily be living on Mars!'

'And this does not worry you?' Solo said smoothly, his heavy lids and thick lashes almost hiding his eyes.

'No, not at all.' Then suddenly Penny realised what she was revealing.

'Ah, the fickleness of women. Why am I not surprised?' he opined cynically, straightening up and taking a step towards her. 'You haven't changed after all.'

As clear as day, the conversation Solo had had with Tina Jenson rang in her ears. She remembered the humiliation, the heartbreak she had felt at the time, still felt, if she was honest. He had some nerve... Talk about the pot calling the kettle... Anger sparked in her eyes as she flung back her head and looked up at him. 'Ah, but I have. I am no longer the little innocent I was at eighteen.'

'I can see that.' Hard grey eyes captured hers in a look of stark cynicism. 'So now young Simon appears to have had his fill of you, and can't help you, you come to me,' he drawled in ruthless mockery. 'Perhaps you and I should explore the possibilities.'

Penny cringed inside, but she could not blame Solo. She had deliberately given him the impression that Simon was her lover, so it was no good being shocked when he believed it, but it still did not prevent her speaking her mind.

'That is a disgusting thing to say.' she snapped.

'But true,' Solo voiced and, with a lightning speed, his hands grasped her by her upper arms and hauled her hard against his long body. 'Once there was something between us.' His dark head swooped, and before she knew what was happening he had covered her mouth with his own in a brutally demeaning kiss.

Penny wriggled furiously, her hands trapped between their bodies, but as the kiss went on she felt herself weakening, old, familiar feelings flooding through her. His hard mouth gentled on hers. His hand slipped to cup the back of her head, while his other hand swept around and up her spine, holding her firmly against his long, lean length. The familiar, masculine scent of him teased her nostrils, and the warmth of his body enveloped her in a seductive cocoon of sensations she had never quite been able to forget.

'As I thought,' Solo drawled, lifting his head, and to her chagrin, while she was breathless and burning up, his slate-grey eyes surveyed her without a flicker of emotion. 'The buzz is still there between us.' His hands spanned her waist, holding her close. 'The question is, what are we going to do about it?'

Humiliatingly aware of her own abject surrender to his kiss while he looked like the original Ice Man, she sought solace in anger.

Scarlet-faced, she spat furiously, 'I don't want to do anything.' She placed her hands on his chest and tried to push him away. 'All I want from you is a straightforward answer about the sale of the house, and that is all there is between us. Either you buy my share, yes or no,' she demanded, with a swift glance up into his hard face, and as quickly away again. He was dark and dangerous, and she must be mad to challenge him.

Solo had to fight hard to keep the knowing grin off his face. The determinedly averted angry green eyes could not hide the flush of arousal on her smooth cheeks or the fact a pulse beat madly in her neck. He wondered what she would do if she knew where his thoughts were really leading, that it was taking all of his famed control not to pick her up and spread her on the desk, and strip her naked.

'Have you finished?' he said.

'That's no answer.'

Solo had been expecting this demand from her ever since he had heard of the death of her parents, but he saw no reason to make it easy for her. Not after the way she had deceived him with Simon. He slid his hands slowly from her waist up over the curve of her breasts and fastened them on her shoulders.

To Penny's horror her breasts hardened against the fabric of her blouse at his insolent caress. 'Let me go,' she said, trying to hold herself rigid, but helplessly aware of her body's response.

Solo felt her shudder, and was content, for now, and moved her gently but firmly out of his way. Then he glanced at the gold watch on his wrist, and back at her pink-tinged face. 'I have to go, my lunch date awaits me. But in answer to your question…' Penny held her breath—at last… But the smile he bestowed on her was totally lacking in humour.

'I have tomorrow free. I will call at Haversham Park and survey the merchandise before I make a decision. After all, four more years of use could have seriously damaged the...' he paused, his cold eyes raking over her from head to toe, before he added... 'structure, don't you agree? I do not want to buy a pig in the poke—I believe that's one of your English expressions.'

The only pig around here was Solo, Penny thought furiously. She was damn sure he had not been referring to the house, but having a dig at her. But she had no choice but to agree. 'Yes, all right. What time?' she demanded shortly.

'Fix it with my secretary. I have to go.' He flicked a dismissive glance her way, then opened a door in the wood panelling. He extracted the jacket that matched his trousers, and slipped it on, quickly followed by a conservative navy striped tie. Then to her astonishment he spun on his heel and left without another word.

CHAPTER TWO

PENNY paced the hall for the hundredth time in an agony of suspense. Twelve-thirty, the time she'd arranged with his secretary, had come and gone and there was still no sign of Solo.

She glanced around the familiar hall, and dejectedly sat down on a wooden seat next to the oak hall table. It was well after two. She had just returned from dropping Brownie off at her friend's house, driving like a bat out of hell in case she missed Solo. Brownie always spent Friday afternoon with her pal, shopping, and stopping for tea, and then the pair of them went to the bingo in the village hall in the evening. With James away it meant that if and when Solo Maffeiano arrived they would be alone in the house, which was not a prospect Penny particularly relished. She had hoped to show him around and out again within the hour, with Brownie for company.

The hurt and humiliation she had suffered the day four years ago when she had discovered the true nature of Solo Maffeiano had never really left her. She had hidden her pain well, and managed with the help of Simon to end the relationship on her terms. But yesterday had taught her a salutary lesson.

Much as she despised Solo for the ruthless, heartless type of man he was, when he had pulled her into his arms and kissed her she had felt the same old fierce physical longing that deprived her of what little sense she had.

She hated to admit it, but she didn't trust herself to be alone with him. Which was a hell of an admission, she thought wryly just as the old iron doorbell rang.

Leaping to her feet, she tugged the edge of her bulky woollen sweater down over her jean-clad hips and went to open the door.

'It's blowing a gale and freezing.' A wet, windswept Solo brushed past her and into the hall, rubbing his hands. '*Dio!* Why anyone lives in England I will never know. The climate is the pits. It is more like March than May!'

Penny could only stare. His black hair was plastered to his head, and tiny rivulets of water trickled down his lean, strong face. He was casually dressed in a soft black leather coat that reached to mid-thigh.

'You've arrived,' she stated the obvious, eyes flaring with anger as she recalled how late he was. 'Almost two hours late. I'm surprised you could be bothered at all.'

With a shrug he divested himself of the coat and dropped it on the chair she had recently vacated. Straightening to his full height, he glanced around the hall, not a flicker of emotion visible on his sardonic features, his glance finally settling on Penny.

'Not the best way to greet a prospective buyer, Penny,' he drawled with a tinge of mockery, then arched one ebony brow in silent query. 'That is, if you have not changed your mind, and still want to unload this place?'

'Yes. I do.' Her innate good manners forced her to respond politely. 'Would you like a coffee? You look cold.' Meanwhile Penny was the exact opposite. Hot... Why did he have to be so gorgeous? She stared up at him, trying to still her racing pulse, but frighteningly conscious of the superb powerful male physique. A cream crew-necked cashmere sweater moulded his wide shoulders and every muscle of his chest in loving detail, snug-fitting black jeans followed the line of thigh and hip.

'Ever the lady. But I would prefer a stiff whisky,' Solo said swiftly, and, as though he already owned the whole house, he walked straight into the drawing room. 'Your father used to keep the best stuff in here.'

'Help yourself,' Penny murmured to his back, following him into the room. 'You usually do.'

'Not always.' Solo said with a wry twist of his lips. 'Pour me a drink, and try to act like the lady you purport to be,' he ordered, crossing to the fireplace and holding out his large hands to the flickering flames.

There was no answer to that, and Penny didn't try. She simply crossed to the drinks trolley and poured a good measure of whisky into a crystal tumbler and handed it to him.

For an instant his fingers brushed hers, and sent an electric pulse the length of her arm.

She snatched her hand away, and moved to sit down on her father's old chair beside the fireplace. Thank goodness she'd had the forethought to light the open fire, and, leaning forward, she threw another log on the flames. She had thought it would make the old place look more welcoming, and perhaps distract from other more obvious faults. But at the moment she hoped he would think her face was red from the fire, and not from heated reaction to his slightest touch.

Fighting for composure, she took a deep breath and glanced up. She found Solo had slumped down in the armchair opposite, his long legs stretched out before him in negligent ease, his elegant fingers turning the crystal glass in his hand.

As she watched he lifted the glass to his mouth and took a long swallow. She saw the tanned throat move, and his tongue lick with relish around his firm lips, and she felt again the shameful pull of his physical attraction. How she was going to get through the next hour, she didn't know, but she had to try.

'Your father always did keep an excellent whisky.' His cool grey eyes sought her wary green gaze. 'Why don't you join me?' he queried, tipping the glass towards her. 'You look like you need a drink.'

'No, thank you, and when you have finished that I will give you the tour of the house,' she said quickly. 'You don't want to waste time. The weather is awful, and you have to drive back to London.' She was babbling, but she was so tense she could not help it.

'I am in no hurry,' drawled Solo, his silver eyes fixed on her in steady appraisal. 'It was a slow drive down, the rain was so heavy visibility was cut to about twenty yards, and, by the look of you, you need to relax.'

Immediately she felt guilty; of course he had driven through a fierce storm. Where were her manners? She got to her feet. 'I never thought—perhaps you would like something to eat? A sandwich, soup, anything?'

Solo finished the whisky and stood up, and, placing the glass on the mantelpiece, he came towards her, pausing only when he was within touching distance. 'No, I'm not hungry.'

Derision glittered in his eyes. 'At least not for what you are offering. Let's go.'

Penny's face turned scarlet. She should not have said *anything*. She was only trying to be helpful, but he obviously thought she was flirting. He could not have made it plainer he didn't fancy her, she thought, drowning in embarrassment. But then why was she surprised? He never had, she reminded herself, and, straightening her shoulders, she swung one hand around the room.

'Well, this is the drawing room, as you can see, nothing much has changed since you were last here except...'

'Purple,' Solo said incredulously, finally noticing the surroundings instead of the woman. 'The walls are *purple*.' His eyes gleamed with wry humour as he stared down at Penny. 'When did this happen?'

'Veronica's taste.' Penny said grimly 'It matched her colouring, she thought.' Determined to be businesslike, she ignored Solo's soft chuckle. 'The dining room next,' she suggested.

'Lead on.' Solo placed a hand beneath her elbow. 'But tell me, am I in for many more shocks?'

She wrenched her arm away. 'It depends on your view of a scarlet dining room, a pink morning room, not to mention a rather virulent lime sitting room. Veronica was a colourful person.' She slanted him a cynical glance. 'As I'm sure you know—I seem to remember she was a friend of yours before she met my father.'

After Penny had split up with Solo she'd had a long time to think over the past and, from countless little digs Veronica had made, she couldn't help wondering just what relationship Solo had had with her stepmother.

His eyes narrowed and his expression became darkly forbidding. 'Veronica was never my friend, an acquaintance at best, but I think you better stop right there, and show me the rest of the place. That is why I am here.'

Penny gave a casual shrug, surprised to find she believed him, but refused to admit she was relieved he had denied knowing Veronica on a more intimate basis. Anyway, what was the use of raking over the past with the man? Best to get rid of him. With that in mind she led the way to the dining room.

Solo assumed the mantle of sophisticated buyer, and he asked pertinent questions as if they were two complete strangers as she showed him around all the rooms on the ground floor.

Penny told herself she was glad, an aloof, businesslike Solo she could deal with; at least she thought so, until she had to lead him upstairs.

'I see what you mean about colour,' Solo drawled with a touch of mockery, walking into the master bedroom and stopping at the foot of the bed.' Knowing your father, I can't believe this bright fuchsia and leopard pattern was very conducive to a good sex life.'

The master suite was horrendous, Penny freely acknowledged, standing a couple of steps behind Solo and glancing around with sad eyes.

A bittersweet memory of another time, when her own mother was alive, and the décor was warm almond and elegant. The bed had been a place to curl up in as a child with her parents on freezing cold mornings. There had been no central heating then.

Veronica had been responsible for installing all the mod cons and the horrendous fuchsia wallpaper, not to mention the *faux* leopardskin bedcover. No one with the slightest taste would like this.

'I'm never going to sell this place,' she thought and didn't realise she had said the words out loud. Not without painting it, at least...

'Ah,' Solo said softly and turned to face her. He had wondered when she would finally admit she didn't want to sell the house, and what she was prepared to do to keep it. 'We get to the truth. I was wondering when you would show your true *colours*.' A steely note crept into his voice. 'I should have guessed you would choose the bedroom.'

Penny stared up at the grim lines of his face, lost in memories of the past; she hadn't the slightest idea what he was talking about.

'It is awful, but I could hunt out the old furnishings, and with a pot of paint it could be okay,' she said distractedly, thinking if she got rid of Veronica's worst excesses they might get a better price for the house. As it was it would make most people bilious.

'Or an interior designer, and a lot of money, my money,' Solo suggested with a cynical smile.

'Well, you could afford it,' Penny snapped as it hit her she really was going to lose her home anyway, whether to Solo or a stranger, it didn't matter. Determined not to let him see how the loss of her home hurt her, she pinned a bright smile on her face and glanced up at him.

'Come on...' She gestured towards him with one hand. I'll show you the rest was what she meant to say, but never got the chance.

A large hand curled around hers, and a lazy forefinger trailed a tingling path across her cheek to the edge of her mouth, where it delicately outlined the shape of her lips. 'Sweet, sexy Penny,' he murmured provocatively.

'Hey, what do you think you're doing?' Penny jerked her head back indignantly, her lips tingling where he had touched, and tried to wrench her hand free, suddenly aware of the intimacy of their position, alone in the bedroom.

'Agreeing with you, Penny.' And the hand holding hers effortlessly wrapped around her back and pulled her close to his large male body. With his other he dispensed with the band holding her hair in place so it fell in a tumbled mass around her face.

After the first shock and her own hair blinding her, Penny began to struggle, and launched a hefty, kick at his shin, but all she succeeded in doing was knocking Solo off balance so he tumbled backwards on the bed, with a dishevelled Penny sprawled on top of him.

'Get off,' she cried.

'I'm not on you,' he drawled sardonically. 'Yet.'

Then with one swift movement their positions were reversed, and Penny found herself flat on her back on the bed, with Solo's great body lying half over her. She struggled wildly in an attempt to free herself, and he let her, restraining her effortlessly with his superior size and strength until eventually she gave up and lay helpless and panting, looking up into his strikingly handsome face.

'Let me go,' Penny demanded, her eyes wide with fear and something more.

'Oh, no.' He smiled slightly, but only with his lips; the grey eyes remained watchful, and slightly cruel. 'This time I am going to sample the goods before I pay.'

'Pay! You mean—you—' She stopped, spluttering, then started again on a rising note of incredulity. 'You mean *me*? You think I am for sale with the house?' she screeched, renewing her efforts to scramble from under him.

Solo stopped her by grabbing her wrists and pinning them above her head in one strong hand, and throwing a long leg over her slim hips. 'I'm accepting your offer, Penny.' His grey gaze was intent on her furious face. 'So long as I get exclusive rights to your body for as long as I want.'

'My offer… My body!' she gasped.

'Yes.' His eyes didn't leave her face. 'Starting now,' he insisted with silken emphasis.

CHAPTER THREE

PANIC-STRICKEN, Penny arched up, trying to dislodge Solo's weight from her body, but it was a futile exercise as his mouth with unerring accuracy covered hers. Forcing her head back onto the bed, and prising apart her soft lips, he began a ravishing exploration with tongue and teeth in a kiss that shattered her romantic concept of a kiss for ever.

Before when he had kissed her it had been a gentle invasion, but now it was a blatantly sensual demand to possess, and to her shame she felt the rising heat of desire scorch through her, heating her blood to fever pitch.

As he sensed her capitulation Solo's mouth softened on hers, and with the tip of his tongue he soothed her swollen lips, before raising his head. Her glorious eyes were dilated with desire and her lips softly parted. She was his for the taking...

Penny drew in a deep, shuddering breath of air. She was so caught up in him she was hardly aware he had released her wrists. And before she could recover from the shock of his kiss his hands slid to her hips and in one swift movement had flipped her jumper up and over her head, and tossed it aside.

'I've waited a long time for this,' Solo opined huskily, his sweater removed in a flash. His eyes bored into hers with undisguised sexual intent.

'No. Please,' Penny breathed, shaken to the core by the devastating awareness of the powerful naked torso looming over her stirring a terrifying weakness in her. She was compelled to touch the hair-roughened chest so that her *no please* sounded weak even to her own ears. But he was not listening. His arm slid around her waist, and arched her slender body off the bed, removing the lacy scrap of bra with a deftness that smacked of long experience.

She spread her hands on his chest in a belated effort to push him away. 'No.'

'You invited me.' His face tightened, and his silver eyes glittered with a deep angry passion over her face and lower down to her firm, lush breasts.

Invited! Was he mad? 'No way,' she cried. 'I don't want this!'

Molten silver eyes held hers 'Your body tells me otherwise.' His gaze dipped sensually over her bare breasts as his long fingers tightened around then caressed her waist.

'You can't,' she whispered hoarsely, a peculiar weakness overwhelming her as she took in his bronzed semi-nudity. 'Let me go.' The blood pounded with increasing excitement through her veins. 'You can't force me,' and even as she said the words she did not really believe he would use his superior strength against her.

At eighteen she had ached for him, and he had controlled her girlish fervour with ease, but now he was unleashing the powerful expertise of his awesome masculinity on her and she had no defence. What little resistance she had left collapsing like a house of cards against his sensual onslaught.

Solo ate her body with his eyes. *Dio* but he wanted her, and he knew she wanted him. It was there in her pouting lips and in the jade depths of her gorgeous eyes. She was sex personified, and the fact she had once turned him down made the prospect of her ultimate surrender all the sweeter.

'I wouldn't dream of it,' he responded silkily, and cupped the smooth, creamy fullness of her breast, and trailed his thumb over the rosy tip, bringing it to rigid life, and watched her helpless, trembling response with cynical masculine satisfaction. He would seduce her slowly, and once he had her begging in his arms he would finally cure himself of the fatal attraction she held for him. She would be a body in his bed like countless others before her—until he tired of her.

Penny did not know what had hit her. One minute she was showing him the bedroom, now she was half naked on the bed drowning in a sea of sensations she did not really comprehend. The hands that had tried to push him away with a will of their own stroked over his satin-skinned shoulders, and when his head moved down to kiss her other breast her whole body shuddered in mindless delight.

'Don't lie, Penny,' he drawled against her hot skin, sprinkling tiny kisses back up her throat. 'You want me as I want you.' Once more he found her mouth, his tongue slipping between her teeth with a seductive sensuality until she forgot she was supposed to be fighting him and welcomed the intimate probing of his tongue with innocent, wild enthusiasm. Her fingers slid around his neck and into the silky black hair of his head, her breasts pressed into the hard heat of his naked chest as he held her closer, and she surrendered to the throbbing need his mouth and hands aroused in her.

So it was a brutal shock when suddenly Solo jerked away from her. Senses swimming, her green eyes wide and wondering, she looked up into his handsome face. Hard grey eyes stared back at her.

'This has been a long time in coming. Now tell me you don't want me.' His mouth curled mockingly, his gaze skimmed cynically over her full breasts, his hand flicking insolently over her rigid nipples. 'Deny the evidence of your own body.'

Penny stared back at him, too stunned to speak, and hating him for deliberately arousing her to a point of mindless surrender, simply to point out the weakness of her own flesh.

'Force does not come into it, Penny,' he drawled, his eyes boring into hers with stark demand. 'Make up your mind. You are no longer an innocent young virgin, so stop pretending and act like the mature woman I know you to be. Admit the need, the desire I can see in your eyes. Yes or no.'

Scarlet-faced, her body throbbing with unfulfilled need, she was vitally aware of Solo's half-naked form, the dark intimacy of the bedroom, and she shuddered, unable to subdue the fierce excitement flowing through her veins however hard she tried.

She had thought herself over him long ago, and she had never considered herself to be a particularly sexual person. She'd had no trouble rebuffing the young men she had dated at university, but now she was forced to face the fact that, where Solo was concerned, he only had to look at her, touch her, and for some inexplicable reason her untried body was perfectly attuned to his. It didn't make sense...

'Your silence is very telling, Penny,' Solo drawled throatily, his grey eyes burning into hers as he kissed each breast in turn, while his deft fingers unfastened her trousers and stripped them and her briefs from her body, and she let him... Hypnotised by his fiercely glittering gaze.

'You want to be persuaded. Very feminine,' he husked. Penny gasped out loud as slowly he slid his hand down over her stomach and swept along the length of her thigh, and then trailed his long fingers sensually down her leg with deliberate provocation. 'Very beautiful, and I'm happy to oblige.'

Penny trembled, mesmerised by the rapt expression on his strong, lean face, and the emotions surging inside her. Then lazily he stood up, and, taking her unresisting hand, he slowly lifted it to his thigh.

'See what you do to me, Penny.' He pressed her hand hard against him, and her palm seemed to burn as she felt the strength of his manhood through the fabric of his trousers.

Fascinated and terrified at the same time, she would have pulled back, but he spoke in a throaty, seductive murmur. 'I need your answer, Penny.'

She gulped and then he was leaning over her; his other hand gently touched her shoulder and lower, her skin burnt. Why me? a tiny voice of sanity cried in her confusion. Why did this one man in the world have this devastating effect on her? Her fingers flexed. Horrified, she realised she was stroking Solo with tactile fingers of desire. Swallowing hard, she jerked her hand back and closed her eyes in mortification at her loss of control.

She did not know what she was, what she had become lying naked on the big bed, every nerve end in her body quivering with tension. She opened her eyes and tried to sit up. This had gone far enough, too far...

Solo was as naked as she was! Penny's stomach clenched at the sight of his magnificent bronzed body, the flagrant proof of his manhood casually revealed. She had never seen a totally naked man in her life, and she couldn't credit the rush of excitement that shivered over every pore of her skin simply from looking.

'Well, what is it to be, Penny?' Solo demanded, his voice deep and full of sensual invitation. His finger curled gently around her shoulder and eased her back down onto the bed. He draped his long body alongside hers and her pulse leapt at the contact of naked flesh on naked flesh. Rising over her, he slid his leg between hers as his mouth came down to claim her lips in a scorching kiss.

'Decision time.' Solo's mouth seductively glided along the curve of her cheek, leaving only a breathing space between them; his glittering eyes held hers, demanding an answer.

For a moment a nerve-jangling fear hit her, but with the heat of his body searing into her skin, and bewitched by the sensual promise in his silver eyes, she suddenly thought, Why not? Why deny herself the experience of making love with Solo? She had always wanted to, from the first time she had set eyes on him. No other man had ever been able to make her feel a tenth of what Solo could with a glance. Whatever happened in the future, at least she would have the satisfaction of knowing she had started with the best, she thought wildly, impulsively. 'Yes.'

One simple three-letter word, and Solo Maffeiano's heart leapt and so did another part of his anatomy. For the first time in his life he was speechless. He looked at the exquisitely beautiful naked girl beneath him and it took all his self-control not to rush. He stroked the elegant curve of her throat, the hollow of her collar-bone, and his fingers trembled.

He shuddered, and Penny was aware of every inch of his huge male body and her own, the beating of his heart, the heat, the pressure of his hips against her inner thighs as he eased her legs apart.

Emboldened, she ran her fingers over his back and felt the contraction of muscle and sinew beneath her touch. She pressed her lips to the strong cord of his throat, tasting the salty tang of his skin. Then she gasped as his hand tangled in the long length of her hair and pulled her head back.

The bronzed skin was taut across his perfectly chiselled features as he fought a savage

battle for control. But his eyes…his eyes burnt
dark as night as he scattered gentle kisses on
her cheeks, her eyes, her nose, and finally took
her mouth.

His mouth searched hers with a sensuous,
building passion and with a wild, uninhibited
delight she responded, her tongue duelling
with his, her hands stroking feverishly over his
broad back, his firm buttocks. She felt the ur-
gent thrust of his body as, with a hoarse groan,
he broke the devouring hunger of their kiss.

His dark head bent to press hot, hard lips to
her throat and lower to her breast, and she
arched in wanton pleasure. Her fingers raked
through his hair and slipped to his shoulders
as he reared up. His hands cupped her breasts,
kneading and pushing them together. His
thumbs teased the rosy nipples, his blazing
eyes watching in rapt fascination as the tips
strained to hard, aching peaks beneath his sensuous manipulation.

'Exquisite.' He groaned and then swooped,
his hungry mouth tasting first one and then the
other in a compulsive, greedy passion.

Penny felt the pulsating waves of sensation flooding through her in ever-increasing force. She clung to him, and cried out when his head moved lower, to kiss her navel, and lower still. He kissed and caressed her slender body with a sensuality, a need that Penny had never imagined possible, and she exulted in the tremors that shook his great frame as she responded, her hands touching him, stroking him, wanting to give him the same incredible sensations.

When his caressing fingers slipped into the soft heart of her femininity, she shuddered violently. Every nerve end in her body was taut with a painful, aching need. She grasped his head and drew him to her, and she kissed him with a hungry, untutored, mindless passion.

Solo wanted to wait, to make it last, but he could not; he had waited years already and her aggressive kiss, the scent, the wet, silken readiness of her tossed him over the edge. A near-violent wave of desire surged through him and, with an animalistic growl low in his throat, he lifted her slender hips and drove forward into her moist, tight core.

Penny cried out, the breath left her body, the need was gone, and only the pain remained. The hand that had curved round his shoulder now hit out at him.

'*Dio*, no,' Solo groaned; his slate-grey eyes burnt into hers and his great body stilled. 'No, relax.' His deep voice caressed her cheek, her mouth as he murmured husky words in Italian, then added, 'Wait, Penny.'

He held her pinned to the bed. His magnificent body still linked to hers in the most intimate way possible. He pressed a soft kiss to her lips, and, easing very slightly from her, he licked the rosy tip of her breasts once more, and then, just as slowly, he moved again.

Gradually she became aware the pain had subsided, and an exquisite sensation of mind-bending pleasure bathed her in wave after wave of ever-building sensual tension. Slow then fast, pause…advance and retreat… He stretched and filled her body and soul, and miraculously her inner muscles clenched around him in ever-increasing need until she was once more mindless, lost in a passionate world she had no prior knowledge of.

Solo's darkened gaze flashed to her bemused molten jade one. She was with him every step of the way, he exulted, the cords and tendons of his face and neck etched in rigid lines of restraint. There was no sensual movement that he did not know, and with phenomenal control he utilised them all. With mouth, hands and body he used every refinement of eroticism to make it good for her, to drive her to the brink.

'Solo,' she helplessly moaned his name, pulsating with the exquisite torture of his possession.

It was his downfall. With one final thrust he drove them both over the edge into a tumultuous climax, his great body shuddering violently, the breath stolen from his lungs.

Penny lay there, the weight of Solo's body still pinning her to the bed, but she didn't mind; she was floating in a bubble of euphoria. This incredible man had shown her what it was to be a woman, and it was beyond her wildest dreams. So this was love; she sighed happily. 'Solo,' she murmured for the sheer joy of saying his name.

'I am too heavy for you,' Solo opined roughly, and rolled off her to lie on his back. He was still reeling from the fact Penny had been a virgin, and when he could think straight again he finally concluded the blond boyfriend she had rejected him for had to have been a fool. The thought cheered him no end.

Deprived of the warmth of the closeness of his body, and stung by his prosaic comment, suddenly Penny felt chilled, her euphoria vanishing as reality kicked in. What had she expected? Avowals of undying love, or at least a little romance.

Instead she was lying naked flat on her back staring up at the ceiling in what used to be her parents' bedroom, having just been thoroughly seduced by Solo Maffeiano, a man she'd thought she hated half an hour ago. She wanted to weep. What had she done?

Panicking, she glanced wildly around and, spotting her sweater, she grabbed it and, swinging her legs over the side of the bed, tried to stand up, but a heavy arm curved around her waist and dragged her back against his broad chest.

'Where do you think you are going, Penny?' Solo levered himself up into a sitting position while keeping a firm hold on Penny. 'We need to talk, *cara*.'

Talk! She almost laughed out loud on the edge of hysteria. But, keeping her back determinedly to him, she managed to say steadily, 'I think it would be better if I got dressed first.'

Solo grinned smugly down at her bent head, his arm tightening around her midriff, his hand splayed under one luscious breast. He hadn't felt this good in years. Who was he kidding? He had never felt this good, ever!

'Are you all right?' he asked, his voice gruff with inexplicable emotion. Lifting his hand, he ran his fingers through the tumbled mass of her silken hair in a gentle gesture. Revealing the perfection of her delicate profile. She *was* shy, and now he knew why.

Solo considered himself broad-minded, a man of the world—he had to be with his parentage, he thought with a tinge of cynicism. He had never been the sort of man who was bothered about his female companions' past affairs. His only rule was monogamy for as long as a relationship lasted. He never asked about past lovers, and by the same token never told.

He let his fingers trail down the long length of Penny's blonde hair, loving the silken feel, the warmth of her small body against his chest, and he had to admit, on a purely primitive level, it gave him incredible satisfaction to know he was her first and only lover. She had rejected him once, but not any more...

'Yes. But do you mind?' Penny said, grasping long fingers that were edging ever closer to her breast, and trying to prise the arm from around her waist. 'You have had your fun, now let me go.'

Solo's arm tightened fractionally. She was doing it again...rejecting him. His silver eyes turned cold grey, and he withdrew his arm from her waist. 'Certainly.' And to Penny's surprise she was free.

Not daring to look at Solo, she scrambled off the bed and pulled her sweater over her head, not caring about underwear, and, finding her jeans on the floor, she quickly pulled them on.

'Why the rush to dress, Penny? I have seen a naked lady before, and I already know every intimate inch of you,' Solo prompted mockingly.

'Thank you for reminding me,' she said with icily polite sarcasm, incensed by his mockery. In her fragile state, she needed reminding she was one of a legion like a hole in the head...

Then she made the mistake of turning to look at him. He was lounging against the headboard of the bed, like some great, smug god of mythology, totally unfazed by his nudity. His magnificent olive toned body made her feel weak all over again. No man had the right to look so damn sexy.

'So polite.' Solo casually slid off the bed and pulled on his boxer shorts and walked towards her. 'But, sex aside, we still need to talk about this place.'

Sex. That was all it was to him, Penny thought bitterly, the most momentous, mindblowing experience of her life, and it was nothing to him. He stood there in black shorts, tall and powerful with the arrogance of a man who had complete conviction in his mastery over the female of the species, his slate-grey eyes staring blandly down at her. Suddenly, amid the chaos of all the emotional highs and lows storming through her brain, the one overriding emotion was anger.

'Why, you no-good, lecherous pig, you deliberately seduced me!' She waved a hand at the horrendous fake-leopardskin-covered bed. 'In that bed, and you dare stand there half naked and say we need to talk, as though it was a flaming board meeting.'

Solo reached out and dragged her hard against him, and plundered her mouth in a deep kiss. Penny tried to bite him, but it was a mistake, it gave him easy access to her mouth, and in moments her slender arms were wrapped around his neck, her slender body arching into his in helpless response. To her utter humiliation Solo grasped her hands from his neck and placed them firmly by her sides before stepping back.

'No more talk of seduction, Penny, we both know it's a lie.' His deep voice held a cynical edge 'Your *come-on* was just that. A come-on.'

Shamed by her instant surrender, she looked at him, the pull of sexual awareness impossible to deny, and something tugged at the edges of her memory. Oh, no! She silently groaned. Earlier she had smiled and said, 'Come on,' but he had never let her finish. Did he really think she had asked him to make love to her? In the next half-hour she had her answer.

'Wait while I dress and we will continue our business discussion over a drink.' Solo's cold, mocking eyes flicked over her tense body and to where her small hands curled into fists at her sides before he added. 'A whisky should hit the spot. It does not look as if anything else is on offer, except maybe a slap on the face,' and he had the gall to laugh at her gasp of outrage.

'I'm going to have a shower. I'll meet you downstairs.' Penny spun on her heel and marched out of the room, blinking rapidly to keep the tears of anger and humiliation at bay, and silently cursing the arrogant devil under her breath as she headed for her bedroom and locked the door behind her.

Her anger lasted until she had a shower, and stepped from the tiny *en suite* back into the room she had slept in all her life. She glanced at the cuddly toys arranged on top of a chest of drawers, oddly at variance with the opposite side of the room where a long desk took up all one wall, with her computer in the middle, and shelves of books above.

Suddenly the catastrophic events of the past two days hit her like a punch in the stomach. Her body aching in places she'd never known was possible, she sat down on the narrow bed and stared around. Her home was no longer hers to keep. James would never know the idyllic childhood she had enjoyed, the timeless sense of belonging. She wrapped her arms around her middle and, doubled over, she finally let the tears fall. How long she sat silently sobbing she had no idea until a knock on the door made her hiccup.

She heard the handle turn, and was glad she had locked the door. Quickly she rubbed her wet cheeks with a shaking hand. The last thing she needed was for Solo to find her red-eyed from weeping and naked but for a towel in a bedroom. She shuddered—whether in fear or remembered pleasure, she refused to acknowledge.

'If you are not downstairs in five minutes, I'll break the door down.'

'Yes, all right,' she snapped back, the cold determination of his tone telling her he meant it. Rising to her feet, she dashed into the bathroom and splashed her face and eyes with cold water. Returning to the bedroom, she withdrew clean bra and briefs from a drawer and a fine blue sweater, and slipped them on.

Solo Maffeiano was right about one thing, she admitted with brutal realism. Sex aside, she did have to talk to him. She stepped into her jeans and eased them up her legs.

Crossing to the mirrored dressing table, she snapped the fastener at her waist, and took a minute to brush her hair back behind her ears. She didn't appear any different, she thought in surprise. Without make-up and with her hair loose, she still looked like a teenager. It was the bane of her life, and why very few people took her seriously. Well, that was about to change as far as Solo Maffeiano was concerned...

Penny pushed her feet into a pair of mules, then opened the bedroom door, a light of steely determination in her green eyes. It lasted until she walked into the kitchen and found Solo leaning against the bench, two cups and saucers arranged before him, and waiting for the coffee to percolate.

'I thought you wanted a drink,' Penny said, refusing to admit she had been surprised to see the sophisticated, super-rich Solo doing something so mundane as preparing coffee, or that the sight of his long body dressed again in black trousers and the cream sweater had the power to make her heart miss a beat.

Shrugging one wide shoulder, Solo turned to face her. 'I decided against alcohol. I want you to have a clear head for our discussion.' His grey eyes met and held hers. 'So there can be no mistakes, or cries of foul later,' he informed her with a tinge of sarcasm colouring his tone.

'As if I would,' Penny denied hotly. How dared he imply she was less than honest?

One dark brow arched sardonically. 'This from a girl who once spent an unforgettable few weeks with me years ago, and then declared it was a mistake.'

Unable to hold his gaze, and without a ready answer, Penny pulled out a chair and sat down at the pine table before raising her head and glancing back at him. 'I can assure you our business dealings will be strictly legitimate.'

A cynical smile twisted his hard mouth. 'We will see,' he said enigmatically, and, turning his back on her, he filled two cups with coffee as she watched. 'Black with one sugar?'

He had remembered, Penny thought, astonished. 'Yes,' she murmured, taking a deep breath to steady her nerves, and when Solo placed a cup and saucer on the table, and held out the other one to her, she managed to take it with a firm hand. Then she took a deep swallow of the reviving brew, and waited.

Penny watched Solo pick up his cup and drain it in one go before placing it back on the table, and could hardly believe that not so long ago she had been naked on a bed with the man.

He was so firmly in control, whereas she felt like a nervous wreck.

He swung a kitchen chair next to hers around, and straddled it, his arms resting on the bowed-back. Involuntarily Penny's green gaze dropped to where his legs were spread over the chair, the fabric of his trousers pulled taut across his muscular thighs, and felt a swift curl of heat in her belly.

'Right, Penny. Haversham Park, and what is to be done with it,' Solo said crisply.

Penny lifted her head, embarrassed at where her wayward thoughts were leading, and, fighting down the blush that threatened, she said equally crisply, 'Firstly, to satisfy my curiosity. How did you acquire a share of my home? I still cannot get my head around the fact my father sold it to you without telling me.'

For years Solo had thought Penny must have been in on the deal he'd made with her father, a deceitful little gold-digger, but now he wasn't so sure. Her dismay at finding she had lost half her home was obviously genuine. But then she had always been a consummate liar. She had led him to believe their marriage had been a foregone conclusion, when all the time she had been waiting for her boyfriend to return. But it left him with the tricky question of what to tell her. The truth wasn't an option; he had no intention of appearing a bigger fool over Penny than he already had.

That last Saturday four years ago, he had formally asked her father's permission to marry her, and had told Julian obviously he had no intention of developing the land around what was his future wife's family home. Julian was disappointed, and hinted he needed money. So as a form of compensation, or, to put it more cynically, the price of his bride, Solo had parted with a large amount of cash and Julian had insisted Solo take a half-share in the house in return.

Solo had had to leave in a hurry, and so he'd been delayed in asking Penny to marry him. When he had returned six days later, he'd been glad he had. Penny had not been around, but Solo had signed the deed with her father while waiting for her.

Then, with Veronica's information that Penny had been at the vicarage with her friend

Jane, he had gone looking for her and found her with Simon. Fury did not begun to cover how he had felt at the time. Rejected and robbed in one week was not something he had ever contemplated happening to him. But it had reinforced the belief he had developed in his youth that women were not to be trusted, with his mother and grandmother as prime examples.

Remembering the fiasco now made his teeth clench. For once in his life he had let his guard down and as far as Solo was concerned the whole damn family had taken advantage of the fact to con money out of him. A half share in a house they had no intention of leaving or selling was of no use to Solo. He had been well and truly tricked.

'Well?' Penny said, the long silence praying on her already-taut nerves.

His eyes flickered, the pupils hard and black, dilating with what looked like anger. For a moment he stared at her, and then suddenly he smiled, his expression bland.

'As you know I bought some acreage from your father with a view to developing it. Your father was quite happy with the price I paid, but he had a very expensive wife in Veronica.'

'Tell me about it,' Penny muttered dryly.

One dark brow elevated sardonically. 'Yes, exactly. Anyway, I had a feasibility study taken on the profitability of the project, and it wasn't viable. Your father was disappointed, because he needed more money. Veronica had very expensive taste, though not particularly good, judging by what she has done to the house.

'Knowing Veronica, I felt some sympathy for your father when he approached me and offered me a half-share of the house as collateral for a rather large sum of cash for an alternative investment he had in mind. I agreed because I felt a little guilty that we were not going ahead with the original project.'

'How very altruistic of you.' Penny said scathingly. 'But that does not explain why he never told me.'

'He was a proud man, maybe he was hoping to invest and make a profit.' Solo shrugged his broad shoulders indifferently. 'Perhaps he was hoping to remedy the situation before anyone knew. But I am sure he would have told you eventually. Even you must admit he couldn't possibly have expected to die so soon.'

That was true enough, Penny thought sadly. Veronica and her father had spent every summer in the south of France, while Penny had stayed home and looked after James. Veronica had always flashed the photographs around to all and sundry of the villa and yacht they'd leased.

'You're probably right.' There was a connection tugging at the edge of her brain, something that she was missing. But with a sigh she gave up. There was no sense in dwelling on what she could not change. 'So you buy me out or we sell,' she said flatly, getting back to the point of the talk.

'No,' Solo's steel-grey eyes met hers. 'There is another choice. In your case it's the only choice.'

'That sounds ominous,' she said, trying for a lightness she did not feel. 'In fact it could almost be construed as a threat.'

'Not a threat, a promise. I promise to restore Haversham Park, and pay all your debts, plus your expenses, and you and James can stay here. In return…'

For a split second hope sprung in her heart. 'You turn most of it into a hotel and leave us with an apartment or something,' she finished for him, thinking with relief that it was an incredibly generous offer.

'Not quite.' Hard eyes stared down at her. 'It stays a private home, you will still run the place, but we share it.'

'*Share!*' she exclaimed, jumping to her feet. An unpaid housekeeper was what he meant, and Penny could imagine nothing worse than sharing a house with Solo, having to see him parade his girlfriends in front of her. 'No way.' She could not bear the idea and she did not question why.

Rising to his full height, Solo let his strong hands fall on her shoulders; she tried to shrug him off, but his hold tightened.

'So impulsive,' he opined hardly. 'But allow me to finish. We get married and you stay here but as my wife for as long as I want you.'

'Your *wife*?' She almost choked.

'Yes,' Solo said flatly. 'Then when we part the place is yours free and clear.'

Her stunned gaze lifted up to his. He had to be joking... His grey eyes stared back cold and implacable, and there was a ruthlessness about his hard, handsome features that told her he was not. The colour drained from her face; she could hardly breathe. Solo was a man who always got what he wanted—she should have remembered that.

A hollow laugh escaped her. Well, he'd already had her, to put it crudely; what had she got to lose? 'Why?' Penny demanded stonily. 'What earthly benefit will it be to you?'

'What do you think? After what we did earlier, how can you ask that?' Solo looked at her, his smile filled with arrogant amusement. 'Or perhaps like most females you are fishing for compliments.' He shrugged slightly, his powerful shoulders lifting beneath the fine cashmere of his sweater, his handsome face expressionless.

'I don't mind humouring you. You were exquisite at eighteen, and the years in between have been very good to you. You have ma-

tured into a stunningly beautiful woman.'
Blatantly he let his eyes drop to her high, full
breasts clearly outlined by her blue sweater.
'My hobby is collecting perfect works of art,
and to my utter astonishment I discovered you
were one of that rare breed of woman, pure in
body, if not mind.' he inserted cynically. 'I
intended to be your lover four years ago, but
you denied me, and I don't take denial easily.
I figured you owed me, and today I collected,'
he declared dangerously, and Penny erupted
into angry speech.

'I owe *you*. You have some gall. I don't
know how you did it but you have already stolen my home—what more can you want?'

'You,' he told her inexorably, his fingers
biting into her shoulders. 'I was surprised to
realise I was your first lover, so naturally I
intend to hang onto you for as long as I want
you.' His eyes glittered with ruthless disregard
and Penny could not believe the colossal arrogance of the man.

She tilted her head back, a light of battle in
her gaze. 'That is the most disgusting, chau-

vinistic statement I have ever heard. You can't own a woman like an object,' she flared back.

'I don't want to own you for ever. A temporary wife was what I had in mind,' Solo said mockingly, and she shrugged in an attempt to dislodge his restraining hands.

Penny shook her head. 'This is surreal. I don't believe I am having this conversation.'

Slowly his eyes drifted over her and her skin heated where his eyes touched. His mouth twisted in a menacing smile. 'Believe it, *cara*,' he commanded just before his mouth settled with deadly accuracy over hers.

CHAPTER FOUR

WHO said lightning could not strike twice? Penny thought inconsequentially as Solo pulled her hard against him, and, from ravishing her mouth, he moved to the soft curve of her ear. Already she could feel the swift flush of heat that signalled her instant arousal, but, now she knew what he could do to her, her body's anticipation was a hundred times more intense. She turned her head to try and escape, but his mouth hungrily followed the elegant curve of her throat, his hands sliding up under her jumper and the wisp of lace that covered her breasts. She moaned as his long fingers expertly teased the hard bud of her nipples, an unbearable spasm of excitement lancing from her breast to the apex of her thighs.

'Why fight it?' Solo demanded with sibilant softness. 'The choice is yours.' Slowly he moved his large hands down to span her narrow waist, his eyes locked onto her dazed

131

green. 'Marry me, or I keep my share in the house. It will make a nice country base when I visit my London office.' Solo living in her home! Penny's mind boggled as he continued, 'And I would prevent you from selling until you go bankrupt and I snap up your share for peanuts. I don't mind either way, your choice.'

She gazed up into his hard face, saw the icy determination in his cold eyes. 'You actually mean it,' she said after what seemed like a lifetime had slipped by. In a way it had, she thought—her life, if she agreed to his outrageous suggestion. 'But what about love in a marriage?' She had to ask; was he really so unfeeling?

'Love is a lie, simply another word for lust believe me. But I never lie about sex.'

'Sex.' Penny looked at him with angry eyes. He couldn't have made it clearer he didn't believe in love. 'That is all this is about for you. Never mind this is my home, and my brother's—my *life*.' Fury mingled with an aching sense of loss.

'And possibly a baby, unless you happen to be on the pill,' Solo cut in bluntly.

'Oh, my God!' Penny exclaimed, the colour leeching out of her face. She had had unprotected sex. 'You—you—bastard,' she said, hitting out at his chest. 'Where was your common sense, your condoms?' she cried. A man like Solo should carry a permanent supply. 'How the hell do I know where you have been? You could have sentenced me to death.'

A violent change came over his features. He grasped her flailing hands in one of his and his other arm tightened around her waist. 'Stop right there.'

His eyes narrowed, a thin white line circled his tight lips, and a muscle in his jaw beat against his bronzed skin. She wasn't quite sure what had happened, she only knew he terrified her.

'I am not such a bastard as to put a woman's life at risk.' Solo was furious, because Penny was right, he should have used protection, he always had before. Only this woman staring up at him with her huge green eyes had the power to make him forget, and he bitterly resented the fact.

'So you say.' She swallowed hard. 'But...'

'But nothing.' His eyes glittered with cruelty. 'I have the medical proof. But you were never the shrinking violet; quite a tease, as I recall. You might have hung onto your virginity, but there are other forms of sex equally as dangerous.'

Penny stared at him in disbelief. 'You think... I...' She was lost for words.

'Not so nice when the shoe is on the foot.' Solo mangled the English saying.

'The other foot,' she corrected unthinkingly.

'Whatever.' His voice hardened. 'But we are straying from the point. You agree to marry me and you get the house. Obviously there will be a pre-nuptial. But any child I keep.'

She stared at him. His expression was unreadable, his jaw hard, his eyes steely grey. He meant every word. He let go of her hands, and they fell limply to her sides. Fear made her knees weak, and she was grateful for his supporting arm, but she knew better than to let him realise it. She lowered her eyes to fix blindly on his chest. If he sensed the slightest weakness, he would take advantage of it. She didn't know how, but he was that kind of man, a predator, and she was his prey, and he had caught her.

Penny thought of James, and any child she might have. It was a real possibility—it was the middle of her cycle, and, the way her luck had been running lately, almost inevitable. Glancing up through the thick fringe of her lashes, she could not deny Solo was a devilishly attractive, virile man.

Once she had loved him with all her heart, and she felt moisture glaze her eyes, and she blinked it away. Now she was numb with pain, hating him for what he was making her do.

'I'll be your lover,' she offered, her voice shaking, and she kept her eyes lowered. She couldn't marry him, not without love.

'No, I can get a lover anywhere, but you may be pregnant. It is marriage or bankruptcy.' His free hand curved around the nape of her neck, and he tilted her head back, forcing her to meet his gaze. 'Yes or no?'

There was no choice. Even if she could persuade him to accept her offer of lovers, what would she tell James? Plus if there was a child, she would rather be married, and if they ever divorced there would be more financial support for any children.

'Yes, all right. I will marry you.'

'A very wise choice, Penny.' His silver eyes flared with what looked like triumph into hers. 'I knew you would see sense,' he concluded with arrogant self-assurance.

It was the arrogance that did it. From feeling like crying, Penny felt like screaming, anger bubbling up inside, and in that instant Penny changed her mind. His dark head bent, he was going to kiss her, but she placed a small hand on his chest. 'No, wait a minute, I've changed my mind.'

She cried out as his hand tightened on her neck. Contempt raw and violent blazed in his pale eyes. 'Already you are back to playing games.' Hauling her against him, he added, 'But no more, Penny.'

'No, you don't understand.' The colour surged in her cheeks. 'I want to marry you.' She looked defiantly into his eyes. 'But if there is a baby it has to be brought up and educated in England, here at Haversham Park with me.'

Something flickered in his eyes, and his heavy lids fell, masking his expression. 'I accept, Penelope,' he said, his deep voice not quite steady.

For a second Penny wondered if he was laughing at her, and if she had just made the biggest mistake of her life, then he kissed her, and it wasn't in the least amusing. He was taking her mouth with a hungry, raw possession, and she didn't care, because if he had been gentle with her she thought she would have cried, unable to stand the pretence. This way it was simply sex...

'Penny,' he groaned her name, his lips softening, gentling on hers.

Maybe not so simple as she was transported back in time to the first time they'd met, in this same kitchen, to their first kiss. She placed her hands on his broad chest, and responded with the same helpless longing.

She whimpered as he slipped his hands under her sweater and she felt his fingers hot on her naked flesh. She looped her arms around his neck. His mighty chest heaved, and then he took her hands from his nape.

'Not yet,' Solo said softly. 'I have too much to arrange.'

All Penny wanted to do was arrange his gorgeous body naked on the kitchen table and, with a guilty flush of colour at her erotic thoughts, she stepped back, avoiding his gaze.

'You said James was on holiday.' He reached out and cupped her face between his palms. 'When is he due back?' he demanded, staring down into her beautiful face.

'Eight days or so,' she murmured.

'That should be fine—and Brownie?'

'It's her bingo night. I drive down to the village and collect her about ten. Why the sudden interest?' she asked.

He looked into her eyes and smiled. 'Because you and I are going to Italy in the morning. With James away and Brownie here to look after the house, it is perfect timing. So pack a bag, and then let's have something to eat. I'm starving.'

'Italy! I can't go to Italy.'

Solo placed a kiss on her brow and set her free. 'You can and you will, but for now do as I say. I need the laptop from my car, and

I'll use the study.' Slanting her an almost boyish grin, he left her standing in the middle of the kitchen totally confused...

Penny sliced carrots and wished she were slicing Solo's neck. What had she done? What did she actually know about the man she had agreed to marry other than she hated him? Solo was a very private man. The first time they were together all she had known about him was that he was a wealthy businessman, and he lived in Italy. She had asked about his family, and he'd told her he was an only child and his parents were long gone, and he had no relatives. Her young heart had filled with compassion and she had kissed him, thinking how awful to be so alone in the world. Now she wasn't so sure, if it weren't for James she wouldn't be in this mess...

Penny gasped, horrified where her thoughts had taken her; for a nanosecond she had actually thought if it weren't for James she would not happily, but willingly, have walked out of her family home, and out on Solo Maffeiano.

She loved her half-brother, and she glanced around the kitchen, the familiar room she had known all her life, the only home James had ever known. She could walk out, but she would still be stuck with a huge debt, and how could she explain to James they had no money, and no home?

Her lawyer's plan for her to sell up and start afresh with James was finally consigned to the dustbin of useless ideas. Solo would not allow it. One didn't need to be a genius to see he could delay the sale for ever if he wanted to. He had the money and the power; he was in complete control.

She shivered, suddenly feeling cold. Gathering up the carrots, she dropped them in the pan with the chopped meat and onions. Solo was used to the finest food. Well, tough!

He was getting beef stew and potatoes.

Washing her hands under the kitchen sink, she dried them with the kitchen towel, and sat down at the table. Penny sighed and stared out of the window, at the overgrown garden, and wondered where her life went from here.

James's and Brownie's futures would be secure, which was a major consolation. They need never know the circumstances of the proposed marriage, never know the happy couple actually despised each other, if Penny was careful. Their lives would not change, except for the better, with Solo's money to make life easier.

Would it really be so bad? she asked herself. Apart from this visit to Italy Solo was insisting on, she might hardly ever see him once she was back. His interests were worldwide; he had told her he didn't get back to his home in Italy as much as he would like. So it was reasonable to suppose he would not spend much time in England.

She let out a breath. Her own innate honesty forced her to admit that being able to keep her own home, having great sex occasionally, and the possibility of a child of her own was not a bad deal. When had she become so cynical? Penny sighed, and, folding her arms on the table, she rested her head. Just for a moment.

The death of her father had turned her life upside down. Then, just when she'd thought she was over the worst of her grief, and was beginning to see the light at the end of the tunnel, Solo Maffeiano had walked back into her life, and turned it upside down again.

She was bone-weary and so tired. Once she had loved Solo so much, marriage to him had been her dream. Now it was her nightmare. Her long lashes fluttered over her cheeks, her breathing slowed, and she slept.

That was how Solo found her. She looked so young, so defenceless, and for a moment he questioned if he was pursuing the right course. He still had not got over the shock of discovering he was her first lover. The blond youth had to have been an idiot, or perhaps with the idealism of the young he had respected Penny too much.

He hardened his heart. Damn it to hell! She had not been that innocent. Penny had quite happily deceived her boyfriend and him... She owed him, and this time there was going to be no mistake. She'd marry him, and like it.

He reached out a hand. His first inclination was to shake her awake, but instead his fingers

stroked gently down the back of her head.
'Penny, *cara,* wake up.'

Somewhere in the distance Penny heard the
softly voiced command, and, eyes slowly
opening, she raised her head. She felt the caress of a hand on her hair and jerked upright.
'Solo, what do you want?' She spoke sharply.
He had surprised her but she could feel a much
more dangerous emotion heating her blood,
something that had to do with the sight of him
smiling down at her.

'Something smells good.'

'Oh, hell! The stew!' Penny jumped to her
feet and dashed to the stove. 'It's nearly burnt.'

Solo laughed and moved to stand close.
'What will you do about it?'

'Nothing—you can like it or lump it,' she
said tightly. 'Sit down, it will be two minutes.'

He flicked a finger down her cheek 'Relax,
I don't mind, anything will do.' He pulled out
a chair and sat down, much to Penny's relief.

Filling the kettle, she moved around the
kitchen setting two places at the table and,
when the kettle boiled, pouring water onto
some dried mash potato.

'Very cordon bleu,' Solo drawled mockingly, eyeing the plate of stew and mash she put before him warily.

'I never said I was a cook,' Penny shot back, taking the chair opposite, and, picking up a fork, she began to eat.

'Then it is as well I am not marrying you for your culinary ability,' Solo said, one ebony brow arching sardonically.

She looked up and suddenly, in a flash of clarity, she realised what had tugged at the edge of her mind earlier, when Solo had explained he had given her father the money against the house. But in the same breath had said it was not a viable proposition for development. Solo was a ruthless businessman—he would never waste money on a loser. But that was exactly what he had done, and was still doing.

She looked up, her eyes flashing. 'No—then why the hell are you marrying me?' she demanded, her smooth brow creased in a confused, angry frown. The deal he had offered her was marriage, and she got to keep the house. But that meant she had been wrong four years ago when she'd thought he was only after her for her home!

For a moment she wondered if she had made the most horrendous mistake of her life at eighteen. Then she remembered the other woman Patricia had told her about and the sound of Solo's laughter and his, 'I'll always love you,' to Tina Jenson, and she knew she had been right to walk out on him.

She searched his hard, handsome face seeking an answer. He was strikingly attractive, he could have any woman he wanted, so why her?

'Let's be blunt,' she said quickly before she lost her nerve. 'I am marrying you for money, but your reason escapes me. I'm sure you have never had to pay for a woman in your life.'

'A compliment, I'm flattered.' Solo said with a wry grin.

'It's not funny.' Penny replied. 'This is my life we are talking about. Is it because I dented your ego once when I said I preferred Simon to you? A touch of old-fashioned revenge?' Not giving him time to respond, she continued, 'I find that hard to believe—we both know you were not that bothered. It certainly isn't because you feel anything for me, and I cannot believe it is just for sex—you are notorious for your women.'

'Stop.' Solo's eyes locked onto hers. 'The past is not up for discussion.' He pushed the half-eaten plate of food away and rose to his feet. 'Suffice it to say I have my reasons, and all you need to know is that the wedding is arranged for three days' time in Italy.'

'Three days, just like that?' Penny shook her head in amazement at his arrogance. 'You say jump, and I say how high?' she said sarcastically.

His hands closed over her shoulders and he drew her to her feet, his dark head bending towards her. 'You're getting the idea.'

'Am I?' She could feel the warmth of his breath against her cheek, and her throat constricting at his nearness. His lips brushed against her mouth and she trembled.

Solo felt her reaction and smiled. 'Oh, yes.' he drawled, lifting his head, grey eyes gazing intently on her slightly pink face. 'Now, if you haven't packed yet, I suggest you do it now, because in an hour poor Brownie will be standing in the rain waiting for you.'

'Oh, hell! The car.' She chewed her bottom lip in angry frustration. She'd left it out, and the old vehicle had a nasty habit of stalling in the rain. 'It is all your fault I forgot.' She jabbed a finger in his chest. 'If it doesn't start you can fix it. After all, you're supposedly the best at everything.' She knew she was being childish, but it was the only defence against him she had left.

'You've lost me.' Solo let his hands drop from her shoulders and stepped back. His own wide shoulders elevated in a shrug. 'I have not touched your car.' He had never met a woman who could switch so instantly from one subject to the next.

But he was grateful because if he'd had to explain why he was marrying her, he no longer knew the answer. He had told himself she and her family owed him big time, and no one got away with cheating Solo Maffeiano. But it wasn't strictly true. Julian Haversham had contacted him and offered to repay half of the money, and the rest when he could afford it.

Solo had refused his offer, and told him he was quite willing to wait. The money wasn't really important, the amount was small change to a man of his wealth.

All he knew was every time he looked at Penny he felt a fierce stirring of lust coupled with the old hatred and contempt he had felt when he had found her in the arms of a young man.

'I know that,' Penny said after a long pause. 'But the car does not like the rain and because you were late I had to rush down and drop Brownie off, in case you arrived while I was gone, and I left it outside. It's not the most reliable—'

'What?' Solo exclaimed, back to the present with a jolt as he remembered the car parked outside. 'You're not still driving your father's old car?' His brows rose in astonishment, when he realised what she was talking about. 'It was ready for the scrap heap years ago.'

'Not all of us are blessed with millions,' Penny replied bitterly. 'And the car is perfectly all right.'

'So long as it does not rain,' Solo said dryly.

She looked up, and saw the amusement in his eyes, and a smile quirked the corners of her full lips. 'Yes.'

'No problem, we will take my car.'

To say Brownie was surprised when a gleaming black car drew to a halt outside the bingo hall and Solo Maffeiano stepped out was an understatement. Penny sat huddled in the front passenger seat on Solo's orders as he said there was no need for both of them to get wet, and watched as he took Brownie's arm and led her to the car.

'This is wonderful news, Penny,' Brownie said, settling comfortably in the back as Solo started the car. 'I could hardly believe my eyes when I saw Mr Maffeiano, but I always thought he would come back.'

What news? Penny was about to ask when Solo cut in. 'How could I possibly stay away from you any longer, Brownie? I really missed your cooking.'

'Oh, Mr Maffeiano.' Penny looked on in astonishment as Brownie moved forward and patted Solo on the back. 'You are such a one.'

It got no better when they were safely back indoors.

'I better explain to Brownie...' Penny started to say, but Solo ignored her.

'You will find a bottle of champagne in the fridge, Brownie. Will you join us in a little celebration?'

Brownie smiled—well, more of a simper, Penny thought nastily.

'Well, I don't usually drink, but for you, yes, I will.'

'For us, Brownie.' Solo moved to Penny's side.

'Wait a minute,' Penny demanded, turning stormy eyes up to him. 'Where did the champagne come from?'

Dark and with a devilish grin, Solo curved an arm around her shoulders. 'I brought it with me, darling, and put it in the fridge while you showered after—'

'Yes, okay,' she cut him off, horrified he was going to tell Brownie how they had spent the afternoon.

He squeezed her shoulder, his smile mocking the blushing confusion she could not hide from him. 'Darling, Brownie must be the first to know we are getting married.'

CHAPTER FIVE

'How do you feel?' Solo asked, his brow furrowed in concern. 'It never entered my head you might be afraid of flying.'

Strapped into a flight seat, one hand gripping the armrest as if her life depended on it, Penny managed to turn her head and glance up at Solo leaning over her.

Trust him to look incredibly attractive and disgustingly fit, while she felt like death. He was wearing a pale linen suit and a white shirt open at the neck. The suit had appeared from the back of his car yesterday along with the champagne and an overnight bag. Penny didn't believe for one moment that he always travelled with a change of clothes prepared for any eventuality as he had said. She suspected he had had a much more sinister reason. If she had not fallen into his arms so easily, she was prepared to bet he would have hung around until she did. He was a devious, manipulative swine at the best of times.

Not that she cared in her present state of health. But to give him his due, Solo had called the flight attendant and demanded some water for her, and impatiently he had vacated his safety seat and walked the length of the private jet to get the water himself, such was his concern.

'I didn't ask to come to Italy,' Penny said between clenched teeth. The water had eased her raw throat a little, but she was sure she was going to be sick again, and she had only been in the plane twenty minutes.

'Open your mouth and swallow this pill,' Solo demanded, his lean fingers reaching for her lips.

'What is it?'

'A travel sickness pill. Just swallow it, you will feel better, trust me,' Solo soothed, stroking the back of her hand that grasped the armrest. 'Try and relax, the nausea will pass.' Meekly opening her mouth, she felt his fingers against her lips as he placed the pill on her tongue. 'Now have another drink of water.'

With a hand that trembled she lifted the glass to her mouth and swallowed, then, feeling cold, she slid down in the seat in a state of near panic. Solo took the glass from her shaking hand and passed it to the male flight attendant, then sat down again.

'Feeling better?' His deep, husky voice was anxious.

'Not so you'd notice,' she tried to joke, but her nerves were shot to pieces. 'I don't like flying,' she said with feeling.

'Why didn't you tell me?' She saw him stiffen, his jawline taut. 'I could have done something about it.' Prising her hand from its deathlike grip on the armrest, he held it firmly in one of his.

'You never asked.' His skin was warm and his grip comforting and Penny laid her head back and closed her eyes, feeling marginally better.

'No, but it's not that unusual,' Solo said soothingly, slowly stroking the back of her hand. 'Lots of people are afraid of flying, but there are excellent medications available to overcome the problem.'

Penny's lips twisted in a wry grimace. Airsickness was the least of her problems. Her biggest problem was the man gently stroking her hand. It was hardly surprising she was ill after yesterday and a sleepless night. She was an emotional wreck before she ever got on the damn plane!

Until three days ago, she had been a reasonably contented woman. Her childhood had been happy until the death of her mother, but she had battled though her loss, and accepted her father marrying again and loved her half-brother. The only blip on the smooth running of her life had been the summer when she had first met Solo and fallen headlong in love with him, or so she had thought...

But with grim determination she had got over what she saw as his betrayal, and gone to university, passing all her exams. The trauma of losing her father and Veronica was fading and she was on the first step of the ladder to being a successful author of children's books. She was quiet by nature, but with an inner core of strength that made her fight against adversity.

That was until yesterday afternoon. Before she had been an inexperienced girl who had not discovered the depths of her own sexuality. But Solo had changed all that in a couple of hours, when he had shown her what it was to be a sexually aware woman. She had been struggling with the emotional fallout ever since.

Last night she had watched him charm Brownie. Then he had stood at her side and listened while she'd rung Jane's mum on her mobile and told her she was going on holiday to Italy for a week, and while she'd spoken with James. Then Solo had called her a coward for not revealing their marriage plans.

Penny had been furious, but later, when he had walked her upstairs to her bedroom, to her shame she had been torn between hoping he would leave her alone, and then, when he'd kissed her goodnight at her door, wishing he wouldn't. No wonder she'd had a sleepless night.

'Penny.'

'Hmm,' she murmured, her eyelids fluttering open.

Solo looked down at her through thick black lashes, an intimate glance that made her heart miss a beat. 'Feeling better?'

As if he actually cared…Penny thought mutinously, but bit down on the childish response and hesitated for a moment, listening to her body. 'Yes, I think I am.' She sighed in relief. The nausea had gone.

Solo sank back in his seat, and breathed in deeply. Thank God she had got a bit of colour back in her face. Not willing to admit seeing her sick and as pale as a ghost had made him feel as guilty as sin. He had bulldozed Penny into coming to Italy with him. But seeing her ill had terrified him. There were times when he wanted to wring her lovely neck for the way she had rejected him in the past, but other times, like now, when he wanted to cradle her in his arms and comfort her.

He must be getting soft in his old age—then he dismissed the thought; age was not something he wished to dwell on. He cast her a sidelong glance. She was resting her head back, the elegant arch of her throat exposed by the open neck of the blue blouse she was wearing, as was the shadowy cleavage of her luscious breasts. He felt a tightening in his groin. What the hell was he thinking of? The girl was ill!

'So, Penny, tell me,' he said, calmly determined to divert his wayward thoughts. 'How is it in the twenty-first century a woman of your age is still terrified of flying? Surely you must have tried to get over your fear before now. I know you and your family fly down to the South of France at least a couple of times a year.'

'There are such things as boats and trains,' Penny remarked, slanting him a wry glance. With her nausea gone, she had time to look around. The cream leather armchairs and the bar all portrayed the wealth of the man at her side. The fact she was still in the safety seat, and had no intention of moving until the plane landed, did not stop her appreciating the luxury the plane afforded.

'But as it happens I've never been to the South of France—it was Dad and Veronica's holiday. They stayed in England for Christmas, but when I came home for the Easter and summer vacations, they took off the next day. It was a chance for them to have a break on their own while I was there to look after James. I've never flown before. In fact, technically you could say I've never been outside of the UK.'

'You have never flown!' Solo declared incredulously. 'I don't believe it. You've never even been abroad?'

'Unless you call the Channel Islands abroad. No…James and I had a week in Guernsey two summers running. It is a nice journey by boat, and there is a lovely beach at St Peter's Port. The weather is generally better than in mainland Britain.'

'I need a drink.' Solo got to his feet. He also needed to think. 'Want anything?' he asked curtly.

'No, I'm fine.' Penny looked up. His eyes burned into hers. He was angry.

Solo shook his dark head in exasperation, and moved to the bar. For years he had naturally assumed Penny had benefited from her father's upturn in fortune at his expense. But now he was not so sure; either she was a great actress, or too soft for her own good.

Unfortunately for him he was beginning to think it might be the latter.

The red dress apart, Penny's clothes appeared to be classic but conservative. Today she was wearing a blouse and neat-fitting navy trousers, suitable for travelling. Her blonde hair was tied back and she looked the same as she had at eighteen. And she had never flown before!

To a man who spent half his working life travelling in his own jet the notion was unthinkable. Plus he had known Veronica, and he could easily believe she would dump her child on Penny and take off to the high life. He was a bit surprised that Julian Haversham had agreed, but then he'd been an old man with a young wife—what else could he have done? That thought brought Solo up cold.

Solo was silent for the rest of the trip, and Penny turned her head towards the window and stared out at the vast expanse of clear blue sky. He was probably angry and disgusted with her for being ill. Served him right if he was fed up with her already. The whole sorry mess was his fault, and on that thought she fell asleep. When the plane slowed and the noise increased, she started awake with a nervous jolt. But she did not have time to feel ill before the aircraft touched down.

Solo unfastened her seat belt. 'I think I better carry you,' he said, his mouth tight.

'No. No.' Penny struggled to stand up, knocking his hand away. 'I can manage, just lead me to a house on terra firma, and a bathroom,' she said with feeling.

Her mouth felt dry, her blouse was sticking to her, and it did nothing for her self-esteem to see Solo looking as cool and elegant as ever.

The customs officer waved them through without even looking at their passports.

'You must be well known,' Penny murmured as they exited Naples airport. Unaccustomed to the heat and the brilliant sunlight, she shielded her eyes with one hand and glanced up at Solo.

But his attention was fixed on a white-haired, casually dressed man in shorts and a black shirt who flung his arms around Solo like a long-lost brother, and a rapid conversation in Italian ensued. Then the older man turned to smile at Penny with sympathy and Solo quickly introduced him as Nico.

When she was seated in the back of an elegant black car, Solo beside her, he explained. 'Nico and his wife look after my home, and they both speak a bit of English, so anything you need feel free to ask them.'

They drove for what seemed miles in silence. With each breath Penny took she was aware of the faint scent of Solo's aftershave. He was too close sitting beside her, his arm casually resting along the back of the seat, his jacket pulled open, and the white shirt did nothing to hide the breadth of his muscular chest.

When the car suddenly turned and she fell against him, she quickly straightened up and looked out of the window, and was glad of the distraction as the car was angling into a concealed driveway flanked by massive stone pillars and lined with trees.

She gasped when the house came into view. 'This is your home!' she exclaimed, turning stunned green eyes to his perfectly chiselled profile.

Amazingly, colour striped his high cheek-bone. 'Yes, it is, and I like it,' he said, his voice hardening almost defensively, and stepped out of the car, opened Penny's door and held out his hand.

A pretty fantasy—there was no other way to describe it. The pale blue stuccoed house, with delicately carved white-painted shutters, had fantastic sculptured scrolls and smiling nymphs at each corner and marching along a stone balustrade at the base of the high slate roof were twelve sculptured figures. In the vast expanse of a paved forecourt were three fountains with elegant dolphins and mermaids. The design was quirky classical, but so *not* Solo…

He was an aloof, arrogant man, and if she had had to picture his type of house it would have been something impressive and solid in granite, with no frills, as hard as he was.

'Penny.'

She glanced up. 'Yes,' she said and, ignoring his hand, she got out of the car and looked around. Beyond the open courtyard there was a terrace with a riot of colourful flowers and shrubs leading to an oval swimming pool. A sloping lawn ended at a row of orange and lemon trees with a view of the sparkling blue sea beyond.

'Do you approve?' Solo asked, moving to stand beside her, and deliberately sliding an arm around her waist to hold her at his side.

'It's beautiful,' she answered honestly. 'But not what I expected.'

'Things rarely are. As I am beginning to realise,' Solo said enigmatically, and urged her towards the porch.

Nico preceded them in and a smiling dark-haired woman of about fifty waited for them. 'My wife, Anna.'

'Welcome back, *signor*, and this must be Miss Haversham. Good morning,' Anna said with a heavy Italian accent.

Was it still morning? Penny wasn't sure— the effect of Solo's hand on her waist, warm and possessive, added to her confusion and, glancing at her wrist-watch, she registered it was almost one. 'Good afternoon.' She tried to smile.

Solo grasped Penny's arm and led her across the marble-floored hall to the foot of the stairs.

'Penny has had a bad journey,' he explained quietly. 'Leave the luggage till later, Nico. I am going to take her up to her room. She needs to rest.'

'Wait a minute,' Penny said as her delighted gaze swept around the beautiful hall, the delicately painted antique Italian furniture. A roll-top desk against one wall, a gorgeous hall table. 'Can I—?'

'No, upstairs,' Solo said firmly and, striding forward, he almost dragged her up the curving staircase, and along a wide landing and into a room.

'Why the rush, I am feeling much better and I would like to have a look around,' Penny said as he released her and closed the door, her angry green gaze clashing with grey.

'Because you have had a very traumatic journey and you need to recover,' Solo said smoothly, walking towards her, his mouth curved in a brief smile, and to her astonishment he walked straight past her.

'Here is your bathroom.' She turned and he had opened a door, and beyond it was the gleam of cream and gold tiles and sparkling mirrored walls. 'Drink your tea, then take a shower and have a rest.'

He was ordering her around like a child. 'Now, wait a minute…' Penny muttered, burning with resentment and other feelings she preferred not to recognise, but, ignoring her, he continued.

'Your dressing room is over here, but don't waste too much time unpacking.' His grey eyes clashed with her rebellious green. 'On Monday you will be moving into the master suite as my wife.'

Wife hit her like a thunderbolt. She glanced wildly around, then back at Solo. He had moved to stand only inches away from her, and it finally registered in her tired mind— Italy, *this* man, *this* room, *this* was reality.

Her head jerked up and she stared at him. 'It's impossible, Solo. You can't get married just like that.' She was panicking. 'I mean, you need documents, a birth certificate, and papers.' She tossed back her head, and hoped he would not recognise her panic. 'What about my family, friends?'

'All arranged. I spent a constructive hour in your father's study. It wasn't possible for us to marry in England quickly. Luckily I have some pull in Italy and I have the documentation.' He was staring at her, his expression unreadable. 'I have an appointment with the relevant authority in an hour, and later today we are going shopping for some clothes for you.'

'There is nothing the matter with my clothes,' Penny cut in angrily.

His grey eyes made a slow, indolent appraisal of her slender form, and she was horribly conscious of her crumpled blouse and trousers. 'Not quite bridal finery,' he remarked, moving closer.

'I don't need you—'

He lifted one finger and pressed it over her parted lips. 'All you need to do is to look your usual beautiful self on Monday, and keep your mouth shut, except to say *sì*.' He looked at her mouth and then into her eyes. 'Everything clear?'

He must have gone through her father's papers in the study, and she had let him, she thought, angry with her own trusting stupidity.

He tipped her head up, and her breath caught in her throat when she realised he was going to kiss her. She told herself it wasn't what she wanted, but when his lips replaced his finger on her mouth she welcomed his kiss with a soft sigh of surrender.

Solo lifted his head and looked down into her dazed green eyes, the softly pouting mouth, and offered, 'If you like we can have a wedding reception for your friends when we return to England.'

'That would be nice,' Penny said rather nervously as she glimpsed the deep, sensual warmth in his eyes.

'Good, because there is no going back,' he mocked. 'You're mine.'

Something Penny was made very much aware of at six o'clock that evening as, stripped to her briefs, she stood in the changing room of an exclusive boutique silently fuming.

She had slept for most of the afternoon. Anna had awoken her with a cup of tea and some very English cucumber sandwiches, and the information the master would be waiting for her downstairs in half an hour. Physically feeling much better, Penny had showered and dressed in a plain rose-coloured shift dress in fine cotton, a matching scarf held her long hair back and, with sandals on her feet, she had made it downstairs in time.

Solo had taken a brief look at her and said, 'Very nice, but I think we can do better than that for your wedding dress,' which did nothing for her self-confidence.

'In that case, you can't come with me. It is unlucky for the groom to see the wedding dress before the marriage service.'

With a sardonic tilt of one ebony brow, Solo said, 'Foolish superstition. A man makes his own luck in this world.'

Solo certainly did, Penny thought wryly, and did not bother arguing.

A short journey in a fire-red sports car saw them arrive at this exclusive boutique in Sorrento. The owner, a stunning-looking woman named Teresa, greeted Solo with a kiss and a hug, while Penny was subjected to a brief smile and a comprehensive examination of her slender figure, before Teresa turned back to Solo and a discussion in Italian followed.

Roughly Penny pulled the cream creation over her head and smoothed it down over her slender hips, her temper simmering. Half a dozen times already she had paraded out of the cubicle into the salon, and had to suffer the indignity of Solo lounging on a satin sofa and studying every inch of her body. Then discussing the relative merits of the garments in his native language with Teresa, before saying yes or no.

At least that was what Penny thought they were doing, but they could have been arranging a hot date for all she knew, and she felt like an idiot. She did not even bother looking in the mirror this time before she marched back out into the salon.

'So will this do?' she demanded, her green eyes flashing fire. Teresa was now on the sofa beside Solo. The woman might as well sit on his lap, Penny thought angrily. It was perfectly obvious they were very good friends and probably more. Not that she cared, she told herself…

Solo's grey eyes lifted, and an arrested expression crossed his hard features. Slowly his gaze raked over her face and down her throat, to her slender shoulders and lower. 'Beautiful,' he murmured.

She felt the heat of his glance down her body, like a flame, and looked down. Then blushed scarlet when she realised the strapless gown, embroidered in tiny seed pearls, revealed the upper curve of her breasts, and fitted like a second skin into her narrow waist and down over her hips to end above her knee. 'There is a jacket to go with it.' She spun around.

'No, wait,' Solo demanded and slowly she turned back to face him.

He had stood up, and moved to stop in the middle of the floor. She glanced up at him, a tall giant of a man with silver-grey eyes, and then quickly lowered her eyes as he slowly walked all the way around her.

She half turned. 'I'll get the jacket.' But long, tanned fingers closed over her shoulders and turned her back to face him.

'Not yet, let me look.' His grey eyes raked over her from head to toe. 'This is the one.' His deep, husky drawl feathered across her nerves as smooth as silk. 'You look incredible,' and, turning to Teresa, 'You agree?'

Penny made her feet move. 'Right, so that is that,' she said flatly, dashing back into the changing cubicle. But she did not escape quite so easily. By the time they left the boutique she was the owner of three formal gowns, a whole load of mix-and-match casual summer clothes, if one could call designer labels casual—the prices certainly weren't—and to her shame some very flimsy underwear Solo took delight in choosing for her.

'Did you have to ask Teresa what she thought of lace thongs?' Penny snapped when they finally got out of the shop. 'I have never been so embarrassed in my life.'

He slanted a mocking sideways glance at her as he led her to an outside table at the restaurant next door, and held out a chair. 'Sit, you're looking rather flushed, and your naivety is showing.' And he had the nerve to laugh.

'Well, I would never wear one,' Penny said sharply.

'Shame.' Solo smiled down at her, a wicked gleam in his eyes. 'I rather like the image of you in a tiny lace thong,' he murmured as he took the seat opposite her.

'You're disgusting.' Her flashing green eyes clashed with his. 'But then at your age I should not be surprised—you probably need all the titillation you can get!' she shot back, deliberately having a dig at his age in the hope of denting his massive ego.

His lips twisted into a cynical smile that held a hint of cruelty and his eyes held no humour at all. 'You're brave in public with a table between us,' he told her blandly. 'But beware of challenging me, Penny. You're a novice in the sexual stakes.'

He regarded her silently across the table for what seemed like an age, and it took considerable will-power to hold his gaze. 'But unlike you I am still young enough to learn.'

With a shout of laughter he threw his head back. 'Have you any idea what you have just invited, you foolish girl?'

'I am neither a girl or foolish,' Penny replied, infuriated by his laughter.

Reaching across the table, he grasped her hand in one of his. 'That could be construed as an offer for me to teach you everything I know.' He lifted his hand to his lips and kissed her palm, and she felt the sensual effect right down to her toes. 'Thank you, *cara*,' and at that moment the waiter arrived.

Penny wanted to rage at the arrogant devil, but, thinking over where her anger had led her, she could see his point.

'Champagne, Penny?'

'Yes, please.' Why not? Maybe getting drunk was not such a bad idea. Face it, she told herself, it is the only one you have left.

His slate-grey eyes raked over her expressive features, pinning her gaze. 'Not a good idea. Alcohol never solved anything. Trust me, I know.'

He was a mind-reader as well; why didn't that surprise her? Letting her lips curl in a brief smile, she taunted, 'You would, oh, mighty one, font of all knowledge, seducer of hundreds of women.'

'I will take that as a joke...this time,' Solo warned with a hint of steel, and she wondered at her own nerve in goading him.

'Have some champagne.' He poured the sparkling liquid into the glass provided. 'A toast to our marriage and us. It can be as happy as you choose to make it, Penny.'

'Why is it up to me?' she asked dryly. 'Unless I'm mistaken, it takes two to make a marriage.'

Solo leaned back in his chair, his handsome face expressionless. 'Because I know what I want from this marriage,' he declared with thoughtful deliberation. 'But I'm not sure you do.'

'I don't actually want to marry you at all. I simply want to prevent being declared a bankrupt and keep a roof over my brother's and my head,' she slashed back bluntly. 'And as you are hardly likely to spend much time at Haversham Park, and I am certainly not going anywhere else, it will be a temporary marriage of hopefully brief duration.' Her life was full enough with James and her fledgling writing career to look after. What the hell! As long as she wasn't pregnant, she could come out of the sorry mess smelling of roses, with Solo the villain. After all, he already had a long-term mistress in Tina Jenson.

Lifting her glass, she pinned a dazzling smile on her face. 'To us,' and she drained the glass. 'But tell me,' she said, placing the glass on the table and glancing across into his flint-like eyes. He was so confident and incredibly attractive, he mesmerised and made her want to murder him in equal parts. 'How did your PA react to your news, or haven't you told her yet?'

One ebony brow arched sardonically. 'An interest in my business? You do surprise me.'

'Well, rumour has it Tina Jenson is something more than your PA,' Penny said with a brittle smile. 'I do hope you have informed her of your forthcoming nuptials, it is only good manners,' she ended facetiously.

His grey eyes became coldly remote on her mutinous face. 'Of course,' he drawled. 'Tina as my PA is aware of my movements at all times.'

Anger hot and instant scorched Penny's cheeks. 'I'll just bet she is.' To think Tina was his lover was bad enough, but to have it tacitly confirmed by the arrogant devil was too much.

He watched her with merciless eyes. 'As for the rest,' he said cuttingly. 'I never listen to rumour, and neither should you.'

'So you never slept with Tina?' The question just popped out and Penny could have kicked herself.

'I didn't say that,' he corrected silkily. 'But it is nice to know you are jealous, Penny, darling.'

CHAPTER SIX

PENNY watched him drink his second cup of coffee with bleary eyes. Solo had eaten a good breakfast, ham, eggs and three pastries, with apparent enjoyment, while she had struggled to swallow one of the delicious pastries. He seemed to be in an excellent mood, his silver-grey eyes smiling at her across the top of his cup.

'I've been in touch with decorators and Brownie, and with a bit of luck by the time we have to return to England at least the paint-work at Haversham Park will not be so bil-ious.'

'You've what?' she exclaimed. 'Who gave you the right to instigate the decoration of my home.'

'Our home, Penelope,' he drawled sardoni-cally.

He was right again. They were seated at a table outside on the terrace, the sun was warm

177

on her bare shoulders. Italy in May was a lot warmer than England and she had dressed accordingly in a cropped white cotton top and a short denim skirt. But suddenly she felt cold. She tilted her chin. 'You should have consulted me anyway,' she flared, her pride stung.

'I didn't think it was necessary. Brownie assured me she remembers all the original colours.' Solo shrugged. 'I thought that would do for now as I remember it being very attractively decorated.'

He had been talking to Brownie behind her back, and that hurt. Solo had taken over her home and now the loyalty of the one person Penny trusted above all others.

'Later we can discuss any alterations that need to be made, perhaps a new nursery.' At her arrested gasp a glint of amusement flickered in his grey eyes. 'You must consider the possibility, Penny, as you so succinctly pointed out we took no precautions.'

'Well, if it ever happens again, you better make damn sure you do.' Penny hated him for stating cold, hard facts. It was all his fault she might be pregnant.

The amusement vanished from his eyes. 'Oh, it will happen again, and again, of that you can be sure,' he stated emphatically, shooting her a penetrating glance. 'As for protection, if the thought of having my child so horrifies you—' his mouth thinned in a tight, ominous line '—I suggest you wait until we see what nature intends this month, and then I will introduce you to my doctor, and you can take the pill.'

If Penny had not known better, she would have thought she had deeply offended him, but she quickly dismissed the idea. He had made it very plain their relationship was strictly sexual, and of a temporary nature. With Tina in the background it could never be anything else. Why the thought depressed her, she didn't dare question.

'We don't have to get married,' she said quietly.

'Yes, we do.' Solo eyed her with cool implacability. 'I was born a bastard and no child of mine will suffer the same fate.'

'I thought your parents were dead!' Penny exclaimed.

'My mother is, she died when I was ten; my father, I have no idea. He was an American sailor, and my mother a whore.'

'That's terrible,' Penny murmured, her tender heart aching as she pictured Solo as a small boy without family. 'I can't imagine not having a home and family.' She lifted green eyes moist with sympathy to his. 'It must have been awful for you.'

'No, it was the making of me. The streets of Naples were my home. As for family, who needs one? Neither your father or your step-mother were particularly kind to you, or you would not be here now. Save your pity for someone who needs it,' he declared callously. 'Yourself perhaps, because you are still going to marry me. The arrangements have been made, and I will not be made to look a fool in my home town.'

Penny said nothing. But the insight into his upbringing or lack of it had a profound effect on her troubled mind. She could not get the picture of a young Solo having to fend for himself out of her mind. He had every material thing a man could want, wealth, power, stunning good looks, a home. A home filled with perfect objects, and who could blame him for collecting only the best, when he had started life with nothing? No wonder he had insisted on marriage, any child of Solo's would have everything the world could provide.

She cast him a surreptitious glance through the thick fringe of her lashes—but would the child have love? He was so cold, so controlled, but, beneath the hard exterior was he capable of love? As a teenager she had once thought so; he had been light-hearted and had made her laugh, for a few short weeks they had had fun... Later he had made her cry. Perhaps it was not impossible to recapture something of the past.

But for the duration of the meal the conversation was limited to generalities.

Later, acting as though he were a tourist guide, Solo showed her around his home. She stared in amazement at the paintings in the main salon. She recognised a genuine Matisse, and her eyes boggled at the exquisite oriental china, the bronze statues.

His collection of *objets d'art* was eclectic, but everything the genuine original. He had not been joking when he had told her he collected only perfect objects. His home was beautiful, and she told him so after leaving a purpose-built gallery that housed modern art, a Picasso and Jackson Pollock just two of about twenty.

'You are like a human magpie, Solo.' She slanted a smiling glance up at him. They were in his study, and even the desk was magnificent, made of polished walnut, and the silver and crystal ink set had no modern use but was perfect all the same.

His lips curled sardonically. 'If by that you think I am a thief...' he gripped her arm just below the elbow, his fingers biting into her flesh '...let me disabuse you of the notion. Everything I have I have bought legitimately, and that includes you.'

Then he pulled her into his arms, crushing her breasts against his hard, muscular chest, moulding her slender thighs and stomach into the rocklike contours of his body. He lowered his head and his hard mouth covered hers.

Penny could not move, so she did the only thing possible and clung to his wide shoulders as he kissed her with a deep, burning, angry passion.

At last he lifted his head and moved back and her legs trembled, her breathing ragged. 'I never meant…' She suddenly realised the insensitivity of her comment with a background like Solo's and wanted to apologise, but he didn't give her the chance.

'Shut up, Penny, and listen.' His chiselled features impassive, his expression was hard. Walking around the desk, he said, 'I have the pre-nuptial for your signature. Read it, and I think you will find I have not robbed you, then sign,' he commanded cynically.

Penny looked warily at the papers he slid across the desk, rubbing her arm—she would probably have a bruise there tomorrow—then picked up the document.

'More than generous,' she said flatly into the long silence and signed it.

Penny's wedding day dawned bright and clear. Anna insisted on doing her hair—apparently she had been a hairdresser in her youth—and swirled the blonde tresses into a fantastic concoction on top of Penny's head. The final touch was a number of tiny rosebuds from the garden inserted in the soft curls.

Penny glanced at her reflection in the mirror, and hardly recognised herself. The strapless dress lovingly clung to her slender body, the tiny pearls glinting in the sunlight. She slipped on the short jacket with the pearl-studded stand-up collar, and she had never felt so elegant. The three-inch high-heeled matching shoes helped.

The ceremony at the civic hall was thankfully brief. Anna and Nico were the witnesses, and half a dozen other people appeared. Solo introduced her but she was too numb with nerves to take in their names. Penny stood still as a statue at Solo's side as he signed the necessary documents, and she took the pen from his elegant fingers and added her own name where he indicated, and it was all over. It seemed unbelievable to Penny that a few words in a language she barely understood had changed her life.

She glanced up at the man who was now her husband looking as cool and remote as ever. Dressed in an expertly tailored pale grey business suit and looking for all the world as if he had just concluded another business deal. Which she supposed in a way was what their marriage was.

Suddenly, as Solo cupped her elbow in his warm palm, and ushered her out into the bright sunlight, a dozen cameras all seemed to go off at once.

In the noise and confusion that followed Penny felt totally lost. Somebody shouted Solo's name and something else in Italian, and Solo chuckled, and the rest went off in peals of laughter. Penny did not get the joke. But then she didn't get much through the meal that followed in a very plush restaurant—the conversation was quick-fire Italian.

'You're very quiet,' Solo murmured during a lull in the conversation. 'Are you all right?' His mouth was close to her ear and she was aware of several things at once. Gleaming silver eyes alight with amusement, and the faintly cynical curve of his sensuous lips, and the gentle touch of his hand over hers on the table. She caught the glint of the gold wedding band Solo was wearing and wondered why he had insisted on them both wearing a ring. 'You look a little flushed.'

'It is rather warm,' she murmured. 'And I have had rather a lot of champagne.' She made the excuse because she could hardly confess she was worried about what would happen next.

Since signing the pre-nuptial Solo had treated her with cool indifference. In fact she had begun to think he had changed his mind. He had made no attempt to touch her or kiss her, and when she had suggested again last night after dinner that they did not have to get married he had looked at her with a sort of lazy possessiveness, and reiterated it was too late to change her mind.

'Not too much. I have been counting,' Solo remarked softly. 'But I think it is time we left.'

'Already?' Penny exclaimed, coming back to the present with a jolt. She glanced around the guests and saw they all seemed to be settled in for a long liquid lunch. 'But what about your friends?'

'Our guests, my dear wife,' he said pointedly, 'can take care of themselves. Whereas I have an overwhelming desire to take care of you,' Solo drawled silkily, standing to his feet. He caught hold of her arm and pulled her up.

Solo said their farewells and thanks in a mixture of Italian and English for Penny's benefit, and instructed Nico they would be away for three days, and began walking towards the door.

When they reached the street a sudden thought made her blurt out, 'Three days— where are we going?'

'A surprise.' Solo opened the door of the sports car and saw her seated before sliding into the driving seat. 'Obviously not far, as your penchant for being sick in an aircraft curtails the choice somewhat,' he mocked. 'I want you fit for our wedding night.'

She ignored his quip about the night ahead. 'But I have no clothes,' she declared.

'Anna has taken care of everything, just relax and enjoy the ride.' He flicked her a glance of mocking amusement. 'I know I shall.'

In the close confines of the sports car she was aware of several things at once. His long, muscular body, the faint scent of cologne mingled with the male scent of him, the gleaming silver eyes, and the faintly mocking curve of his sensuous lips. She shivered and closed her eyes, battling against the strange fascination this one man aroused in her.

She opened them twenty minutes later and glanced out of the window 'Oh, my God, no! You can't drive down there.' Penny grabbed Solo's arm. 'It's a cliff.'

'Trust me.' He slanted her a grin, his typical macho excitement at the drive ahead obvious. 'I know what I'm doing.'

'God save me from would-be racing drivers,' she murmured and squeezed her eyes shut, and did not open them again until she felt the car come to an abrupt halt. Warily she looked out of the window again, and saw only water.

'Where are we?' She turned to Solo but only his jacket and tie lay on the seat. He was already out of the car, and in a moment was holding the door open for her. Penny climbed out and the heat struck her. She slipped off her jacket and looked around, and looked again.

It was a complete suntrap. A tiny bay at the foot of a cliff with a small what looked like a log cabin perched on the very edge of a rocky outcrop, with a wooden deck and jetty reaching out a few yards into the sea. A small boat rested clear of the waterline on about twelve yards of beach. She turned and tilted her head back and looked up at what looked like a sheer cliff face, until she spotted the serpentine track cut into the rock.

'You drove down that?' Penny flung out a hand and cast Solo a horrified look. 'You must be mad!'

He briefly caught her hand and pulled her around before flinging out his arm in a wide, encompassing gesture. 'Look around you. Beautiful, no?' he demanded in a slightly accented voice, and, not waiting for an answer, added, 'The first time I landed on this bit of sand I was like you, scared stiff at the sight of the cliffs, but now I love it.' A satisfied grin softened his tone. 'The perfect hideaway, no television, no telephone.' He started walking towards the cabin.

The image of Solo afraid of anything was something Penny had trouble picturing. He seemed indomitable. She watched his confident stride, the movement of his buttocks as he walked, and a sudden rush of heat that had nothing to do with the bright sunshine flooded through her. Quickly she moved forward and stumbled in her high-heeled shoes.

'Sugar!' she exclaimed, and in a moment was swung up in Solo's strong arms. 'Put me down.' She tried to wriggle out of his hold, her jacket and shoes falling in the process.

'Stop it unless you want us both to take a dip in the sea,' Solo said dryly, pulling her closer and walking on, ignoring her struggles with an ease that was galling as he elbowed open the cabin door.

'Alone at last, Penelope,' Solo drawled mockingly, lowering her gently to her feet. He was so tense it took all his considerable self-control to speak normally. He wanted to tell her she was exquisite, he wanted to throw her on the bed, and feast on her beautiful body with eyes and hand and mouth. The brush of her body against his thighs as he set her on her feet was agony. He had never wanted a woman so much in his life. 'You like the place?' he asked quickly, but the question wasn't casual.

He had discovered the tiny bay as a child of eight. He had set out to sea in a rubber dinghy he had found on the beach at Naples, even at that age desperate to escape the gutter and a mother who he'd known would never miss him. The dinghy had deflated, he had swum until his arms had ached and had finally been washed up in this bay, and it had saved his life.

Then there had been only the ruins of an old fisherman's cottage and a rotten jetty, the place long since deserted, but it had become Solo's refuge. Whenever the city had got too much for him, he'd walked the miles from Naples and scrambled down the cliff path. Later, when he'd had money, he'd bought the land, built the cabin, and had the track cut out.

Solo could feel some of the tension seep from his muscles as he glanced around the familiar room; it was his sanctuary. He glanced down at Penny. It didn't matter if she didn't like it, he told himself, but for some indefinable reason he knew it did.

Penny's eyes skimmed around the room, and it was just one room. To one side of the entrance door was a kitchen and dining area that took up a quarter of the space. At the other side of the door a long sofa beneath a window, on the next wall an open fire, with bookshelves loaded with books either side. On the far wall, a large bed... She stood rooted to the spot, unable to move a step forward if her life depended on it.

'It's tiny,' she declared hollowly. Her stomach began a series of somersaults as she was struck by nervous dread at the thought of the three days alone in *one* room with Solo. No escape from his overwhelming masculine presence morning, noon and night... Penny glanced up at him. 'There is a bathroom?' she demanded, tension making her clip the words.

So she didn't like it. So what? 'Of course.' Solo frowned, indicating a door to the left of the kitchen area, his expression stern and remote. 'All the facilities are located through there.'

Penny raised an eyebrow. 'Thank God for small mercies.'

'I am not completely primitive,' he said coldly.

'That's a matter of opinion,' she muttered under her breath, and, without a word, he slid an arm around her waist and pulled her hard against his long body. His head bent and his mouth closed over hers with brutal savagery, forcing her lips apart in a kiss that shocked her into numb submission.

'That is primitive, my sweet wife.' Solo's eyes narrowed in a slow, raking appraisal of her slender form. 'You need to know the difference, because what happens next is your choice, but don't try my patience. I waited four years for you, and then another four days— symbolic maybe, but too long.'

She tilted back her head; her eyes, flashing with anger, clashed with his darkening gaze. 'Very symbolic—four is the number of the devil in Japanese culture,' she shot back defiantly.

'Then as you have labelled me a devil, you silly girl...' he grasped her chin between thumb and forefinger, and she could see the cold fury in his silver eyes... 'I am quite prepared to act like one. I would hate you to be disappointed,' he declared with mocking cynicism, his other hand sweeping around her back, and before she knew it his fingers had swiftly unzipped her gown.

'I am not silly or a girl.' She slapped his hand from her face and jerked free. 'You saw to that,' she hissed, burning with resentment and trying to grab at the front of her dress.

'And you loved every minute of it,' he declared sardonically, and, catching her hands, he held them wide, and to her utter humiliation the pearl-strewn gown sank to pool on the floor at her feet.

She heard his sharply indrawn breath and for a long moment he simply stared. 'I have been longing to do that since the first moment I saw you in that dress.' Solo's voice lowered to a husky murmur as his eyes roved over her delicate features and lower to her firm breasts, the tiny waist, and the small white lace briefs that barely saved her modesty.

Struggling to free her hands and burning with embarrassment, she used the only weapon left to her and lashed out at him with her foot, connecting with a shin-bone. But in seconds she was powerless to move as he linked her hands behind her back in one of his, hauling her hard against him and raking his other hand through her hair, sending rosebuds careering to the floor. 'Let me go,' she gasped, wriggling ineffectively in his grasp, the atmosphere suddenly raw with tension.

Solo laughed softly. 'Never.' His silver eyes held her furious green gaze, his teeth gleaming in a devilishly menacing smile. 'And you don't really want me to.' His gaze flicked down to her breasts heaving with her recent exertion, and back to linger on her slightly swollen lips, and then her hair.

'Your hair should always be loose.' Threading his fingers through it, he smoothed the silky mass down over her shoulders in an oddly tender gesture. 'That's how I always picture you.'

A warm tide of colour washed over her body—that Solo pictured her at all was a surprise to Penny, given the women he had enjoyed, and she was rather flattered at the thought. His face was close and there was something mesmerising about his silver eyes, his deep, husky voice.

She felt his hand at the nape of her neck, urging her head back as he lowered his own, and he brushed her mouth with his with an almost reverent gentleness, so different from what had gone before that she sighed her relief, the fight draining out of her. Her eyes fluttered closed as with practised expertise he kissed and caressed her silken skin until every cell in her body pulsed with aching need.

She felt herself being swept up in his arms and deposited on the wide bed, and the soft warmth of silken sheets at her back.

'That's better, my beautiful bride.' And Solo's warmth was withdrawn.

Better for whom? Her eyes flew open. Solo had shed his shirt, and was stepping out of his trousers. With fast-beating heart, she stared at him; his bronze body, all taut muscle and sinew, left her breathless. She gulped. 'What are you doing?' she cried inanely, casting him a nervous glance.

'Well, if you haven't guessed by now,' Solo drawled, his silver eyes gleaming wickedly, 'your education is sadly lacking,' he mocked, and he had the nerve to chuckle as he lowered his long body on the bed and curved an arm around her shoulders. 'But no matter, I will soon rectify your lack.'

'You have a vastly inflated ego,' Penny snapped back, his mockery infuriating her again, but the sight of his naked body had a debilitating effect on her anger. He was even more beautiful, more awesome than the picture that had haunted her sleep for the past few nights—incredibly handsome and with a body to die for. The trouble was she knew just how he could make her feel; her temperature was already shooting off the scale at the warmth of his naked thigh against her own.

'No, merely a vast experience with the female sex.' A smile quirked the corners of his mobile lips. 'Which I am putting completely at your disposal, Penelope mine.'

He was teasing her—the devil thought his vast numbers of lovers were amusing! Penny tore her gaze from the latent sensuality in his grey eyes. 'I am not yours; in fact, I think I hate you,' she grated, not for a second admitting she was also madly jealous at the thought of all his other women.

'You know the cliché: hate is akin to love, but at least hate is an emotion.' Solo loomed over her, supporting his weight on one elbow, but his hand still curved round her shoulder. With his other he held her chin, his silver gaze burning into hers, his expression solemn. 'Indifference is the real killer, Penny, I know.'

For a second a fleeting shadow seemed to dim his glittering eyes, and Penny had the odd idea the powerful domineering male she had just married looked vulnerable. Quickly she dismissed the idea. Solo was a typical Alpha male, and she doubted if anyone, male or female, could ever be indifferent to him. Whether it was love, hate, admiration, envy, lust or jealousy, he aroused strong emotions simply by being Solo Maffeiano.

'And whatever else you are,' his deep, husky voice continued temptingly, 'you are not indifferent to me, Penny, *cara*.' His thumb and finger brushed down her throat, and lower until his palm cupped her breast and the tantalising fingers tugged very gently at the nipple. 'My bride and soon my wife.'

Penny did try to resist, but his touch ignited a burning hunger within her she was helpless to deny. Warmth coursed through her veins, and with a low, inaudible groan, her eyes wide and luminous, she stared up at him. *Wife*, and he was her *husband*. Why deny her own feelings? She wanted him, and which emotion fuelled the craving she did not care any more. Instinct told her despite her naivety that Solo would be a hard act for any man to follow.

Reaching up, she traced the hard line of his jaw with her fingers, and up into the silken black hair at his temples. The marriage might be for all the wrong reasons, and, if she were not pregnant, would almost certainly be brief. She had no faith in her ability to keep and hold a man like Solo, even if she wanted to, but for now he was her husband.

'My husband.' She murmured the words out loud, and he grasped her hand and pressed a hot, hard kiss into her palm.

'Yes. Oh, yes,' Solo said huskily, and her eyes widened into huge pools of helpless longing as he lowered his head. His lips traced her own with incredible tenderness, exploring and teasing and urging her response. 'We can dispense with these.' He raised his head and she felt his hand peeling her briefs from her body. 'I want you naked against me,' he rasped. This time Penny reached for him.

She ran her fingers through his hair and urged his head down. She gave a shaky sigh and parted her lips, her tongue seeking the hot interior of his sensuous mouth. She felt his great body shudder against her, and suddenly he moved onto his back, leaving her stunned, and screaming with frustration.

'I want to take this slow,' Solo rasped, his breathing heavy. 'It's your wedding night.'

Why should he dictate the pace? He dictated everything else, Penny thought in a wild bid for independence. Pushing up, she leant over him, her mouth briefly seeking his before withdrawing teasingly and nipping at his lower lip. Fierce, primitive pleasure swept through her and she was caught up in a desire so intense nothing else mattered. She eased back and deliberately trailed her long hair over his wide shoulders, glorying in her feminine power over him.

'*Our* wedding night,' she amended, and bit lightly into his shoulder, her slender hand stroking through the soft, black body hair of his chest, her fingers scraping over a pebble-like male nipple with tactile delight.

Her green eyes wide and wondering, she traced the arrow of black hair that angled down to his groin, fascinated by his aroused flesh. Her body quivered in delight at the capitulation of his. She wanted to touch him, taste him, wallow in his masculine beauty, his virile power, and Solo let her for a while...until her pink tongue touched the vulnerable velvet skin.

Then suddenly, with a husky growl of need, he pushed her onto her back, held her hands down by her sides, and kissed her with a wild, passionate hunger that melted her bones. She trembled, the blood flowing hot and thick through her veins, as he trailed his lips down to the gentle swell of her breasts and with sensual delight he suckled each one in turn. She writhed as his mouth began an evocative journey to discover every pulse point, every erogenous zone, with an expertise that made every atom of her being spark with incredible heat.

With the air scented with sex, their breath mingled in a branding kiss as they lay, silken skin on skin.

Finally Solo knelt between her thighs. 'You're mine, Penny, my wife,' he said with an animalistic growl of triumph, and then in one deep thrust he possessed her. Penny arched up to him, her fingers digging into the flesh of his shoulder and his side, anything she could cling to as he drove her on and on into an explosive sunburst of heat and light.

'Good morning, Penelope.' Penny tried to stretch, and came up against a hard male thigh; she opened her eyes, and saw Solo grinning down at her. Her whole body blushed scarlet as the events of the night came rushing back.

'Did you sleep well?' Solo asked, his hand slipping beneath the silk sheet to curve around her breast.

Catching his hand with hers, she looked up into his handsome face. Black curls fell over his broad brow and a five o'clock shadow darkened his strong jaw, making him look tough but endearingly dishevelled. 'Not much, as you very well know.' There was no point in denial; they had made love countless times through the night.

His silver eyes gleamed down into hers with wicked amusement. 'Well, we could stay in bed a little longer, if you are still tired.' And they did.

Three days later Penny stood and watched as Solo locked the cabin door and walked towards her. It had been the most perfect three days of her life. They had gone swimming naked in the sea, and made love on the sand, taken out the boat and gone fishing with Penny demanding Solo put back any fish he caught. He had dropped one on her and then washed the fish smell off her in the shower, or so he had said, but it had just been an excuse to make love again.

She looked around the tiny bay, a tear forming in her eye. And she finally admitted what she had subconsciously known all along: she loved Solo, always had and probably always would, but she would never dare tell him. She was his only for as long as he wanted her body, and the tear fell.

'Ready, Penny?' Solo's long arm wrapped around her waist and turned her around to face him. 'Hey, what is this?' He flicked the solitary tear from her smooth cheek.

'The thought of the flight back to England.' She sighed. 'And I was wondering if I will ever get back here again, it is so beautiful.' She told him half the truth.

Solo looked at the woman in his arms, and his heart expanded in his chest. Penny did like his sanctuary. 'Of course you will.' He kissed the tip of her nose and led her to the car. 'If I have to I will drive you back and forward to England, whenever you want.' In fact he would drive to the ends of the earth for Penny.

The ludicrously emotional thought made him stop in his tracks and he let go of her. Solo knew himself that it was only with burning ambition and ruthless self-discipline that he had become the successful man he was today. Emotion played no part in his life.

'Solo…' Penny laid a hand on his arm. He looked ill—he had gone white beneath his naturally tanned complexion, the skin pulled taut across high, arrogant cheekbones. 'Solo…' Ice-grey eyes surveyed her, and every nerve in her body tensed.

'Get in the car, Penny.' he said harshly. What had he done? She hated him, she was only with him now because he had given her no choice and she needed his money to keep her young brother and that damned old house.

It irritated the hell out of him that from the moment he had seen her he had wanted her with a fierce, consuming hunger that had nothing to do with logic, but everything to do with lust. It angered him that he who had always prided himself on the ability to control his passion couldn't control it with Penny.

Her wide green eyes were staring warily up at him; her lush lips, still swollen from early-morning love-making, trembled slightly. He reached out a finger and traced the soft curve of her breasts revealed by the blue sundress she was wearing, and saw her catch her breath. He could take her now; without conceit he knew he was a good lover and he had taught her well. He had never met a more wildly responsive woman in his life. Penny was like a kid in a sweet shop, but he recognised it was because sex was new to her, and what was worse he also knew that her need was nothing like the wild hunger that ate at him.

Shrugging off the unpleasant truths, he dropped a light kiss on the top of her head and helped her into the car. What did he care why she was with him, as long as she shared his bed? he told himself, and frowned as he started the car, no longer sure he believed it...

CHAPTER SEVEN

'ACTUALLY, flying is not all that bad,' Penny said. Anything to break the tension that had sizzled between them since leaving the cabin. She glanced at Solo as he manoeuvred the sleek black car through the traffic. 'Those tablets really worked.'

'Good—in that case you can travel with me sometimes,' Solo remarked, flicking her a side-long look.

'No,' she said immediately, panicked by the thought. 'I couldn't, there is James. And the house.' She had enjoyed the last few days in Italy, in fact more than enjoyed. She cast a surreptitious look at Solo's classic chiselled profile, and her heart ached.

Who was she kidding? She had loved their brief honeymoon; she loved Solo. He had the power to make her heart leap with a single look. But she knew she could never tell him, because she could never forget she was not the only woman in his life.

'We can hire a nanny, staff—it won't be a problem.' His grey eyes were enigmatic with a glimpse of something else less easy to define as they briefly focused on her. Anyone but Solo and she would have thought it was a silent plea. Which was ridiculous. She straightened in the passenger seat.

'No,' she said again. 'I stay at Haversham Park with James, that was our agreement, and you do as you like,' she reminded him with biting sarcasm. 'Anyway, you have Tina to accompany you on your travels; three is a crowd.'

'As you wish, my dear wife,' Solo drawled sardonically. 'But whatever you may imagine, Tina is not my lover, and be advised I will not tolerate anything except complete fidelity on your part, and I will accord you the same distinction as long as the marriage lasts. What you choose to think is your prerogative, but I will not be the subject of idle gossip, understand?' he warned implacably.

He had surprised her by his declaration of married fidelity; whether to believe him or not, she was not sure. As for his distaste for gossip, he was a vastly wealthy, powerful man. A very influential force in the world's money markets, governments listened to him, but as Penny was beginning to realise he had an exaggerated desire for privacy.

She recalled her surprise at first seeing the secluded villa that he called his home, and the amazing little wood cabin where they had spent the last few days. He obviously loved the place and yet he owned some of the most perfectly situated, luxurious hotels around the globe.

Recalling his confession about his mother, she could understand his fierce protection of his privacy, but in this day and age Penny did not believe it mattered. It certainly did not matter to her, and she opened her mouth to tell him so. But one glance at his grim expression was enough to make her close it again, and keep her mouth shut for the rest of the journey.

The difference was amazing. Brownie met them at the door, and insisted on showing them around all the ground-floor rooms. Everywhere had been painted and polished and scrubbed. 'I can't believe all this could happen in less than a week.' Penny turned shining eyes to Brownie. 'You must have worked like a slave.'

'Not a bit of it.' Brownie laughed. 'Mr Maffeiano hired over twenty people. It was wonderful, all I did was order them around.' Turning to Solo, Brownie added, 'And the new bed arrived this morning. You and Penny pop on up and have a look, while I get the lunch.'

Solo took Penny's hand. 'Come on,' he said curtly and led her upstairs.

'What new bed?' she murmured, her pulse racing at the warmth of his hand enfolding hers, and inexplicably she felt nervous. It was stupid, she knew, given how they had spent the last three days. But somehow knowing she loved him had made her more cautious, not less so. Solo had seemed to change as soon as they'd left Italy and he was once more the aloof, powerful businessman. Looking around her now, back in the house where she was born, she felt their sojourn in Italy was quickly becoming a distant fantasy.

In the master bedroom the garish colours had vanished, replaced by the colours she remembered from her childhood. The only difference was a large four-poster bed with elegant cream silk drapes tied back with twisted golden tassels. A thick, quilted cover in the same material and colour, with huge plump pillows, adorned the bed.

'Incredible.' Penny sighed. 'How did...?' She looked up. Solo was standing by one of the long windows, his back to her, and there was something about the set of his shoulders, a tension in his tall frame as he slowly turned around, that froze the rest of the words in her throat. As he walked towards her she was struck again by his superb animal magnetism, an intrinsic male dominance that fancifully reminded her of some lethal predator intent on devouring its prey.

'So was it worth it, Penny?' Solo asked, the words a barely concealed taunt.

'Was what?' She looked at him, mystified.

Solo saw the puzzlement and the slight darkening of her glorious eyes as she watched him approach, unable to hide her sensual response. But that was all it was, he reminded himself. His anger at her rejection years ago had faded, lost in the passionate abandonment of their love-making. But today her refusal to even consider travelling with him, and then walking into this house had brought back to him all too vividly the real reason she was his wife: money and the threat of pregnancy, and it angered the hell out of him.

A self-derogatory smile twisted his sensuous mouth. He had deluded himself into thinking a few nights with Penny in his bed and he would get her out of his system. But the violent, primeval passion he felt whenever he looked at her, or touched her, he knew was the reaction of the primitive male animal in him that lurked beneath the thin veneer of civilised sophistication he presented to the world. She was his mate, only his, and he wanted to keep it that way.

It was not a realisation he was comfortable with. She had bewitched and beguiled him with her mixture of innocence and sensuality, so that he only had to look at her to feel like a randy teenager again. He stared down at her, and gestured with one elegant hand around the room. 'All this,' he drawled, and, closing his hand around her slender wrist, he added, 'This house for my money.' A cynical smile curled his beautiful mouth. 'My body, my bed.'

Penny stared at him, genuinely shocked and then angry. 'I could ask you the same. But I would not be so crude,' she returned.

'Ah, of course, you are a lady...' Long, tanned fingers moved caressingly on the tender skin above her wrist. 'But to answer the question you are too polite to ask,' he said mockingly, 'so far you are repaying my investment admirably.' His ice-grey eyes flared, then narrowed on her angry face, and suddenly she sensed just below the calm surface was a violent rage waiting to escape. 'The highest-paid whore in the world could not have done better,' he opined in a deep, dark voice that slashed through her body like a knife.

A deep flush overlaid her pale skin. It had been insensitive of her to call a man with Solo's background crude, but his response shamed and horrified her. Now she knew what Solo really thought of her, and she collapsed on the side of the bed, only dimly registering that her legs were shaking.

'But I think it is time for another instalment,' Solo suggested, and, roughly hauling her up hard against him, he took her mouth in a fierce, brutal kiss.

'Don't.' She struggled against him. 'Solo…' He was frightening her.

'Yes, say my name,' he breathed, the violence in his eyes making her shake, and she pushed hard at his chest. 'Remember who you belong to.' He laughed, a harsh, cruel sound, and captured her mouth with his own as he tumbled her back on the bed.

The breath whooshed out of her body. 'No, please, Solo,' Penny cried and grabbed a handful of his hair to pull him away. 'I didn't…' was as far as she got.

He lifted his head and the scorch of his laser-like gaze burned into hers as he claimed her mouth again with a low, agonised groan that seemed to reach right into her body and pluck out her heart.

She tried to struggle, striking out at his chest. 'Wait.' Fear, stark and debilitating, made her shudder as his eyes, hard as flint, clashed with hers. One strong hand caught the hem of her dress and dragged it up around her waist.

'I don't need to. I might be crude but you are bought and paid for,' he snarled, and his lips came crashing down on hers again.

Penny battled to breathe, her fingers curved into his shoulder, her other hand pulled his hair, but slowly the heat, the hungry passion of his mouth got to her as only Solo could. His body, hard and taut with a need he could not hide, slid between her thighs, and the hand that pulled his hair turned to caress the silken locks.

'Dio!' Solo suddenly exclaimed, lifting his head. 'What the hell am I doing?'

She saw a flicker of vulnerability in his hooded eyes and her heart squeezed. Solo was the most arrogant, indomitable male she had ever met and yet... Something made her slip her arms around his back and hug him as he would have moved off her.

'I can make a guess,' she tried to tease, staring up into his sombre face, but he wasn't amused.

He jerked to his feet and glanced down to where Penny lay sprawled on the bed and gave her a long, brooding look, before spinning on his heel and walking away.

Penny watched him depart with sad, puzzled eyes. She saw him rake his hand through his hair as he went through the open door, but he didn't look back. The honeymoon was definitely over.

Slowly Penny dragged herself up to a sitting position, and made an attempt to smooth her dress down over her legs. He could not have made it plainer the marriage was to be a short-term affair. Solo was a man who thrived on challenge; maybe she had been too willing and he was tired of her already. Then there was Tina…

A deep, shuddering sigh shook her. How long could Penny live with a man, love a man, when he treated her like a whore he'd paid for? What about every time Solo left on business— would she wonder if he was sleeping with his mistress? His avowal that he demanded strict fidelity in a relationship she had a suspicion should have ended in a caveat. *With the ex-*

ception of Tina. Penny could not live like that; it would destroy her.

Why had she let it happen? Because she loved him, her heart cried.

Dinner was a quiet affair. Penny, dressed carefully in one of the new gowns Solo had bought for her as a kind of armour against her raw emotions, tried her best. She made herself smile for Brownie's benefit and drink a toast in champagne.

Solo sat grim and brooding all evening and it was a relief when he said he had some work to do and she could escape upstairs to bed.

After showering and slipping on a scrap of blue lace that Solo had bought for her, Penny crawled into bed and fell into a restless sleep.

Her eyes fluttered open, a strong arm pulled her gently towards the warmth of a hard male body. 'Solo...' Penny murmured his name dreamily.

'I was a boar earlier, forgive me.' She felt his lips at her temple and then the warmth of his breath at her earlobe, before seeking the soft bow of her mouth, in a kiss of incredible sweetness.

'Yes,' she breathed. A large hand traced up her spine and held her close to the muscular strength of his torso, and the kiss went on and on. She was boneless, floating in a sea of sensations, as long fingers stroked her breasts, the negligee sliding away.

Her lips parted and drank from his, and she felt his slight intake of breath before he moved down to the base of her throat and lower to suckle the small, tight nipples. She moaned softly and ran her fingers along the arrowing hair that spread down past his navel, her touch finding him.

Solo moved over her, his mouth finding hers again as his body took possession with a fierce passion that she met and matched, crying out as she climaxed in a tumultuous explosion of release.

She almost said she loved him but changed the words to, 'I love…the way you make me feel,' just in time.

'The feeling is mutual, *cara*,' Solo rasped, and sucked hard on her nipple, his hands lifting her hips as he thrust ever deeper to the very portals of her womb. Sweeping her through her climax, something she had never thought possible, and on and on until his great body shuddered in wave after wave of violent pleasure, and Penny convulsed around him again in a mutual relief.

They collapsed on the bed, Solo sprawled on top of her, their ragged breathing the only sound, and then Solo murmured something in Italian and rolled off her. He curved her possessively into the hard heat of his body, nuzzled her neck, and she wrapped an arm over his broad chest, her head on his heart, and in moments she was asleep. She woke up a long time later to a knocking on the door, and Brownie calling her name.

'Come on, sleepy head, your husband has been up for hours working, and James will be arriving back in about an hour,' Brownie said with a smile, and walked to the bedside carrying a coffee tray.

Wriggling under the covers into her nightgown, she sat up, and reached out and took the coffee-cup Brownie offered. 'Thank you, Brownie, but you really should not be running up and downstairs after me.'

'Your husband offered, but I told him I wanted you out of bed, not kept in it!' Penny blushed, and Brownie chuckled. 'What a man!' she said and, with an admonishment to hurry up, left the room.

'Penny, I'm home.' James ran into the hall, followed a few steps behind by a breathless Patricia.

Bending down, Penny swept James up in her arms and gave him a fierce hug, moisture stupidly blurring her vision. 'Hello, darling.' She pressed a kiss on his chubby cheek. 'I've missed you.'

Small arms wrapped around her neck, and he said, 'I missed you, but guess what? I can swim!' His beaming smile flashed out. 'Can we go to a swimming pool, Penny, can we? I want to show you.'

'Of course we can, darling, but not right now,' she said with a chuckle, depositing him on his feet. 'Say thank you to Patricia. Brownie is in the kitchen with your favourite...cake.' Before she had finished the sentence James had darted for the kitchen, screeching at the top of his voice, 'Thank you. Brownie, cake, cake, cake.' She watched him go with a shake of her head.

'I hope he wasn't too much trouble,' Penny remarked, glancing at Patricia.

'No, it was a breeze—he got on great with my little terror. But, hey, you are looking good. Mum told me you were going to Italy for a week, and it seems to have agreed with you. I told you, you needed a holiday, and I was right.' Patricia stopped, an arrested expression on her face. 'When did this happen?' She pointed to the newly painted hall.

'Yes, well...' Penny blushed scarlet '...about that...'

'What is all the noise about?' a deep voice demanded, and Penny silently groaned.

Turning slowly, she watched as Solo, wearing black jeans and a short-sleeved black shirt, his great body exuding an aura of almost lethal male sexuality, moved towards her. 'James is back.' She smiled tentatively. After his moody behaviour yesterday and their passionate, almost loving reconciliation in bed last night she

was not sure how he would react, but she need
not have worried.

'Ah, that explains the noise.' Solo smiled
into her eyes, touched his mouth briefly to hers
and whispered, 'Good morning, *cara mia*.' His
eyes gleamed with the smug, sensual satisfaction of a man who knew he had satisfied the
woman in his life. Slipping an arm around her
waist, he turned her to face their guest, easing
her against his long length, her bottom fitting
snug against his thighs, and it felt great. 'And
this is?' He paused, politely smiling over
Penny's head at Patricia.

'Solo Maffeiano. What the hell is he doing
here?' Patricia exclaimed, her eyes out on
stalks. 'I thought I told you to get rid of him
years ago.'

'Please, Patricia, let me explain.' Penny felt
the sudden stiffening in Solo's long body and
abruptly he let her go, stepping to one side.
The feel-good factor had not lasted one morning. Penny almost groaned aloud her frustration, and, glancing up, her green eyes were
captured by narrowed grey ones.

'I don't think I know your friend, Penny, darling,' he drawled, his hard, dark face expressionless, but only a fool would fail to detect the steel beneath the silky smoothness of his voice. 'Introduce me.'

Now would be a good time for the floor to open and swallow her, Penny thought dryly, tearing her gaze from his, but one look at Patricia's bossy, big-sister-type expression, and then back to Solo's icy one, and she knew she was in trouble with both of them.

'Solo, this is Patricia Mason—Jane and Simon's older sister. Patricia and her child were on holiday with James and her parents,' Penny began to explain.

'Never mind the social niceties,' Patricia said. 'What is he doing here?'

'I live here,' Solo said with a sardonic arch of one dark eyebrow in Patricia's direction. 'And as far as I know I have never met you.'

'Well, you have once,' and she mentioned a première in New York. 'And I know all about you,' Patricia fired back. 'I told Penny—Lisa Brunton is a friend of mine.'

'And?' Solo prompted icily. Penny sensed the increased tension in his mighty frame, and slanted a brief glance at his chiselled profile. She saw his jaw tighten and a muscle jerk in his cheek; he was livid.

'Stop it, both of you,' she cut in firmly.

'Yes, let's have a coffee and be civilised.' Solo's hand snaked out, and his fingers dug into Penny's waist as he fixed her with a piercing glance that sent a shiver of fear down her spine. 'I do not want to see my wife upset.'

'Wife? You're married!' Patricia exclaimed. 'To him?' She waved a hand at Solo. 'I don't believe it.'

'Believe it!' Solo drawled. 'Penny and I were married last Monday in Italy, and I have to thank you, Patricia. If your family had not taken James on holiday, it might never have happened,' he ended with a mocking, cynical smile.

The sound of a car horn echoed in the fraught silence. 'Oh, damn—I have to go, they are waiting in the car.' Patricia frowned at Penny. 'But I'll talk to you later.' And, spinning on her heel, she left.

'You can let me go now,' Penny said bluntly. 'I think you made your point with Patricia.'

'Your friend is of no importance to me,' he opined in a flat, chilling voice, turning her to face him, his strong hands spanning her waist. 'But she obviously has a vast influence on you.'

'No, I hardly ever see her,' Penny said truthfully. The last thing she needed was to get into a discussion on Patricia. 'She lives in America.'

Solo's eyes rested thoughtfully on her taut face. 'Your ex-boyfriend Simon is her brother.' His lashes drooped, hiding any sign of emotion in his grey eyes. 'Cast your mind back, Penny—was she in England the first time we met?'

A hot tide of colour surged up into her face. 'She did visit to show her parents their first grandchild,' she said to somewhere over his left shoulder.

'And you listened to her gossip,' Solo prompted, jerking her closer, his hands tightening on her waist. 'What exactly did the woman tell you, *mia sposa*?' He kissed her angrily. Heaven knew what would have happened next if James hadn't appeared at the moment.

Penny had never been so grateful for an interruption in her life. James ran into the hall, his mouth covered in chocolate, and skidded to a halt at the sight of Solo.

'You let go of my Penny.' He stuck a sticky hand on Solo's jean-clad leg.

'What the devil—?' Suddenly Penny was free, and Solo dropped gracefully down on his haunches. 'You must be James. I knew you when you were a baby, and I can't believe how big you have grown.'

'What you doing with my sister?' James asked, not to be deterred.

'Kissing her,' Solo grinned at the little boy. 'I know you love Penny very much, but I love your sister as well, and it is a lot for Penny to look after this big house and everything else, so I am going to live here and help you both.'

Penny was horrified. She had not thought how she would tell James she was married— she doubted he understood the concept—but she certainly would not have started with a lie. Solo did not love her. If only it were true, Penny thought with a stab of longing, staring down at the two dark heads so close together.

'Can you swim?' James asked with the single-mindedness of a child.

'Yes, and I have a house with its very own swimming pool where we can all go on holiday.'

'I've just been on holiday.' James grinned. 'And I can swim.'

'In that case we must build a swimming pool here, maybe in the basement, so you and I can practise swimming together—'

It was outright bribery. 'Hold on—' Penny cut in, but was stopped by James.

'Can we really have a pool?' James turned glowing eyes up at his sister, and she hadn't the heart to say no.

It was as inevitable as night follows day, Penny thought ruefully a few hours later, sharing a pot of tea in the kitchen with Brownie. James was completely captivated by Solo, and surprisingly Solo was extremely good with the little boy.

He had carefully explained he and Penny were married, husband and wife, as James's parents had been. James had pondered for a while and then decided it was okay. Which might have had something to do with discovering Solo had, not only a great car, but a boat and plane as well. Penny glanced out of the window, and at the moment Solo was showing James the engine of his car.

'Alone at last,' Solo said as he walked into the bedroom, just as Penny exited the bathroom wearing a blue towelling robe and nothing else. James had soaked her as she had given him his bath and put him to bed, with Solo looking on. She had left Solo reading James a bedtime story, and had hoped to be washed and changed before he had finished, but luck was not on her side.

'It is almost dinner time,' she said jerkily.

Solo, in a few lithe strides, crossed the room and wrapped a hand around the back of her neck. 'I am sure Brownie will not mind waiting. James is asleep.' His voice dropped to a sibilant softness. 'And you and I are going to have a talk, a long talk about what your so-called friend Patricia told you four years ago.'

'I don't know what you're talking about.' Penny looked straight at his broad chest, unable to meet his shrewd gaze; she had been dreading this moment all day. Solo was no fool, he must have guessed immediately after Patricia's unthinking outburst this morning there was more to Penny's rejection of him years ago than she had admitted at the time.

'You're a hopeless liar,' Solo taunted. 'Your pulse is racing.' He drew her closer, and her nostrils flared slightly at the familiar male scent of him. 'You're as nervous as a mouse with a cat on its tail, and you know you really want to tell me.'

'I am not,' she snapped back, her green eyes flashing up to his. She did not appreciate being likened to a mouse. 'And I've forgotten anyway.' He held her gaze for a tense moment, and, although his expression did not alter, she sensed a hidden threat.

'Okay,' Solo said lightly. 'Then I'll ask your friend myself tomorrow.' She was lying and he had a damn good idea why. She had listened to the poisonous Patricia's gossip and stuck with young Simon. 'She's staying at the vicarage, I believe.' And he watched with savage satisfaction as colour flooded her skin.

'No… Yes. Oh…I don't want you upsetting my friends; I have to live here,' she said quickly.

There was a long moment of silence. 'Not necessarily,' Solo finally said coolly, and he allowed his hand to slip around the front of her throat and graze gently over the swell of her breast. 'We could live in Italy, James as well, of course.' His slate-grey eyes narrowed on her beautiful face, and he waited for her response, tension riding him.

Penny jerked back out of his reach, heat swirling within her, prickling through her breasts until the peaks pushed achingly against the cotton of her robe. Flustered and completely missing his point, she muttered, 'Then you get this house for your damn hotel. You must be joking.'

Solo's shoulders squared, his hard face an expressionless mask. Penny would not move an inch for him, never mind a country. Her friend must have done a real hatchet job on him, and he hated gossips almost as much as he hated liars. 'I never intended turning this house into a hotel. Architecturally it is a perfect gem, and I appreciate perfection. It would be a desecration to alter it. So if you really believed I wanted it for a hotel, then you're a fool.'

Struggling for composure, she looked at him, resentment fizzing inside her. 'No, otherwise you would have bought me out when I offered,' she had to concede. But he was so damn arrogant it would do him no harm to hear some home truths. Why not tell him? Deflate his enormous ego a notch or two.

'But I did believe once you wanted me so that you could get my house. Four years ago when I mentioned your name to Patricia as my boyfriend, she suggested I make sure you were not going out with me simply to get your hands on my home. You see, she recognised your name and told me all about you. A confirmed womaniser.' Penny was getting into her stride. 'You romanced a friend of hers, Lisa, for ages, then dumped her, by my reckoning a week after you met me.' She saw Solo's face darken like thunder but he made no attempt to deny her assumption—on the contrary.

'Lisa knew the score—it was mutually beneficial when I was in New York, nothing more, and it was over the day I met you.'

'For whom, I wonder?' Penny scorned. 'You broke the woman's heart. Jewellery was mentioned as a get-lost gift. Apparently that's a habit of yours.' She didn't see the angry narrowing of his eyes; she was on a roll.

'Never mind the fact you already had a long-time married mistress in Tina Jenson, who was the purchaser of the jewellery, as you obviously haven't got time between women to do it yourself,' Penny drawled sarcastically. 'If I remember correctly, Patricia's final comment was you were far too old for me.' Only then did she lift her eyes to his, and what she saw there made her take a step back.

'And you believed her?' He clasped her wrists, his fingers like manacles around them. '*Dio*, you had some opinion of me.' Fury did not begin to describe the flash of white fire in his eyes, but as quickly it vanished, his features becoming an iron mask.

'Are you saying she lied,' Penny prompted.

'Not exactly, but I'm a lot older than you. What did you expect—a blow-by-blow account of every woman I had before I met you?'

'No, I didn't, I don't,' she blurted, hating him for making her appear a naive young fool. 'I doubt if you could even remember them all.'

'Maybe not.' A cold, cynical smile curled his firm lips and he tightened his grasp on her wrists. 'But I do remember four years ago Patricia's brother was your so-called boyfriend. Did it never occur to you she might have had an ulterior motive in gossiping about me, to protect her brother's interest?'

'No.' She grimaced and tried to tug her hands free. 'Because he was never my boyfriend. He was just a convenient excuse at the time when I discovered what a rat you were, and you're hurting me.'

Solo saw red. His whole life he had been alone and fought for what he wanted. But the one brief moment he had allowed himself to consider a wife and family and reach out to

Penny, idle gossip had destroyed it. Penny hadn't trusted him, and Simon had been nothing more than a decoy.

'Hurting,' Solo snarled. 'You don't know the meaning of the word. I would like to break your elegant neck.' Instead he pushed her away from him. 'I should have guessed.' He shook his dark head, his narrowed gaze raking over her contemptuously. 'No man could go out with you for years and not take you to bed; you're sex on legs.'

'He was a friend, I was crying on his shoulder when you turned up. He was in the right place at the right time,' Penny explained.

Solo smiled tightly. 'For whom, I wonder?' he drawled mockingly, quoting Penny's earlier comment about Lisa, and, tilting her chin with one elegant finger, he said softly, 'Not to worry, Penny, darling, we have each other— for a while.'

CHAPTER EIGHT

SINCE Solo had walked back into this house five weeks earlier, her life had changed dramatically. Penny stared sightlessly at the computer screen. James was fast asleep and she was in her old room trying to work, but her troubled mind would not let her. Solo was in New York and she missed him dreadfully. A sad smile twisted her lips, she loved him with every fibre of her being, but she could never tell him.

Solo had been great with James, and had managed to charm every one of her friends and acquaintances at the party they had held the weekend after they'd returned to England.

Luckily Patricia had returned to her husband in America before the party, but not before she had subjected Penny to a long and detailed questioning over the telephone, ending with the words, 'I hope you know what you are doing, Penny. It is bound to end in disaster.'

Well, her relationship with Solo hadn't. Yet! He was the perfect husband, to the rest of the household, and courtesy itself to Penny. It was only in the privacy of their bed at night he changed into a demon lover. A lover she could not resist. She was like a drug addict hungering for the taste of him, and the more she had, the more she wanted. Sometimes, lost in the wonder of his love-making, she could almost believe he cared, and other times she was filled with shame at her helpless response, her almost blind obedience to his mighty will.

After today it had to stop, she told herself adamantly; she had more to consider than herself now. Determinedly she focused on the screen; she was going to need her work and the money she could earn more than ever.

'So this is where you hide.' A deep, dark voice vibrated though the silence of the room.

Penny swung around in her chair, her startled gaze flashing to the tall, dark figure of Solo standing in the open door, and her heart lurched. 'You're back!' Simply the sight of him turned her on. He had shed his jacket and tie somewhere, his white shirt was open at the neck and his pleated trousers hung low on his lean hips. His black hair had escaped its usual sleek style to fall in wayward curls over his broad brow, and he looked dishevelled and less arrogantly assured than when she had last seen him. They had been married over a month and he had been away for the past four days.

'Miss me, did you?'

Yes—yes—yes! her heart cried. His face was taut, his silver eyes darkly shadowed as they captured hers. For the first time she noticed that his stunning features were tightly drawn and he actually looked tired. She had an incredible urge to simply throw herself into his arms, but instead, with her gaze remarkably level, she said, 'I thought you were away for a week.'

He gave an indolent shrug. 'I managed to finish my business quicker than expected.' He walked across to where she sat at her computer and slanted her a wickedly seductive smile. 'And decided to spend the night with my wife, so you can stop fooling around with the computer, and fool around with me.'

She clocked the time on her computer—it was almost midnight. Briefly she closed her eyes; she was tempted, very tempted. Involuntarily her tongue slipped out and ran over the fullness of her lower lip, but his arrogant assumption she should drop everything for him riled her no end. The past four days apart had made Penny take a long, hard look at herself and she did not like what she had become: a slave to her senses. 'How was your trip?' she asked stiffly.

His dark eyes gleamed with mocking cynicism. 'Polite convention at all cost.' His lips twisted sardonically and he let his gaze wander over her slender body. 'A little more wifely enthusiasm would not go amiss.' His eyes narrowed fractionally on the computer screen. 'What is that?'

Wifely enthusiasm! He made her sound like the little woman sitting at home, and it annoyed her. 'It is the draft of my latest children's book, the second of five I am contracted for,' she told him proudly. 'Contrary to what you think, I do not sit around waiting for some man to provide for me. I do work; I do have a career.'

'I know.' Hard hands caught hold of her arms and she gasped as he lifted her to her feet, and he chuckled. 'Poor Penny. James showed me weeks ago the book you had written. I was wondering how long it would take you to tell me yourself,' he admitted dryly.

Penny winced. 'Am I that transparent?'

'No, not at all,' he murmured wryly. 'You are like me in that respect, very good at hiding things. For instance, I came back tonight because I couldn't keep away from you a moment longer.'

Her green eyes widened in surprise on smouldering grey. It was not a declaration of love, but it was more than he had ever offered before, Penny thought wonderingly. Then his mouth closed over hers in a kiss of breathtaking hunger, his arms enfolding her, and she was left in no doubt he had missed her by the hard strength of him against her thighs.

'Hmm,' he drawled a long time later, giving her a scorching look. 'The master suite—or your childhood bed looks very tempting, and much nearer,' he opined with a husky groan.

Winding her arms around his neck, her whole body alive with excitement, she glanced teasingly up at him. 'The master suite,' she declared adamantly. 'You're a tough guy. I'm sure you can manage.'

'Remind me to exact due punishment later,' he threatened, swinging her up in his arms and carrying her from the room.

He did not need reminding—with deft hands he stripped her naked and laid her in the centre of the wide bed. 'Don't move,' he said in a deep, firm voice, and, standing up, he yanked off his shirt. 'I want to look at you.' He quickly stripped off the rest of his clothes, his heated gaze raking over her body the whole time.

Penny was transfixed; he was more beautiful, more magnificently male every time she saw him. Restlessly she moved her legs, her senses dizzy with desire.

'No.' He grasped her ankles and sat down on the side of the bed, his body angled towards her, and with tantalising slowness he pulled her closer. His silver eyes lingered over every inch of her, the lush, firm breasts, and flat stomach, until his strong hands curved the back of her thighs.

She sucked in a breath, her stomach clenching as he eased her leg over his lap and moved the other around his back, exposing her in every way. His heated gaze devoured her as his thumbs tracked her inner thigh and opened the velvet-soft flesh, brushing the throbbing centre of femininity. She groaned and his dark head swooped to lick and nip across the taut peaks of her breasts.

One hand reached for his shoulder and the other the tempting length of him against her thigh. 'No, not yet.' He slurred the words against her skin as he lavished kisses down over her stomach.

She was on fire, wild with excitement and yet shocked by the blatant eroticism of her position. She wanted to scream and beg him to stop, but her molten, shuddering body made a liar of her. Her back arched violently from the bed. Solo twisted and, grasping her ankles, placed them on his shoulders as he surged inside her already climaxing body. Grabbing her hips, he thrust deep and hard until he finally exploded, spilling his hot seed inside her.

They collapsed flat on the bed, satiated, and Solo murmured, '*Dio!* I needed that,' and, rolling onto his back, went out like a light.

Penny couldn't sleep. Her mind would not let her. He had forgotten the protection again, she realised, and sighed softly—not that it mattered any more… But Solo did not know that, and for a man as coolly controlled as Solo it was surprising. She had meant to tell him she was pregnant as soon as he returned—a visit to her GP yesterday had confirmed it—but one kiss from his beautiful lips and, as usual, sensation took over from sense.

Turning on one side, she gazed down at his sleeping form. He was flat on his back, one arm flung across the other side of the bed, the other above his head. Jet lag, probably. But even worn out he looked incredibly sexy. His hair rumpled, his thick black eyelashes resting on his bronzed cheeks, his sensuous mouth parted ever so slightly in sleep. The tiredness she had noticed earlier had gone, his striking features beautiful and younger somehow in repose.

Her gaze dropped lower, to his great nude body, and she groaned as her gaze moved slowly lower to where even at rest his magnificent sex tempted her touch. She swallowed hard, the memory of the incredible pleasure his body could bring her heating her blood all over again.

She lifted her hand towards his thigh and, with a stifled groan of shame, she flopped back down on the bed, and wriggled back into her nightdress, as if that would stop her wayward thoughts, and closed her eyes tight shut. When had she become such a sex addict she would actually contemplate waking a sleeping man?

Stop it, she ordered her erotic thoughts. Tomorrow she would tell Solo she was pregnant, she decided firmly. Their marriage might have been for all the wrong reasons, but that did not mean they could not make it a success.

Penny loved Solo, and he wanted her, he had come back early, and admitted as much, which was a good start, she told herself. In time he might love her, and in the meantime they would both love their baby. Solo would make a great father; one only had to watch him with James to see that. With her decision made, Penny fell into an exhausted sleep.

The distant ringing of a telephone echoed in Penny's head. She murmured and her eyelids flickered. She heard voices and slowly opened her eyes.

Her sleep-hazed glance slid across to the other side of the bed. It was empty and Solo was standing naked a foot away with a mobile phone in his hand.

For a moment she wallowed in the luxury of studying his tanned back and firm buttocks caught in the rays of the morning sun shining through the window. She stretched languorously and felt a tiny curl of heat ignite in her belly. Yes, today she would tell him they were going to be parents, and that she loved him...

Then she heard his voice. 'Yes, Tina, I know we only returned yesterday, but I want to go to Mexico. Under the circumstances I think it is necessary.'

Penny closed her eyes, ridiculously hoping to shut out the sound. Solo was talking to Tina and all of Penny's new-found determination of the night before to try and make her marriage work took a nosedive; jealousy, fierce and primitive, made the bile rise in her throat.

'Arrange the flight and get down here, as soon as possible. I'll be waiting for you. *Ciao, cara.*'

Penny squeezed back the sting of tears, the heat in her belly turning to nausea. Her eyes flew open. She knew enough Italian to know he had the gall to call Tina *darling* in front of her, and anger hot and swift flooded through her; she looked at him, her eyes on a level with his thighs.

The fiend was physically aroused! With a gasp of outrage she shot off the other side of the bed and dashed for the bathroom, locking the door behind her. She fell to her knees in front of the toilet bowl and was quietly, wretchedly sick. The strap of her nightgown cut into the flesh of her arm, and, shoving it back on her shoulder, she raised her head.

The door handle was turning. 'Penny, *cara*,' Solo drawled. He had the nerve to call her darling as well—the lying swine!

'Why have you locked the door? You can't still be shy.' She heard the amusement in his tone, and felt sick again. 'I need to talk to you. I have to leave soon.'

Rising to her feet, she crossed to the vanity basin and washed her mouth out before answering. 'I'll be out in a minute.' There was no way she was telling him she was pregnant now and, slipping on a towelling robe, she walked back into the bedroom.

He was still naked, but there was a subtle difference that didn't surprise her in the least. She looked up at him with hard green eyes. 'You wanted to say something.'

Solo's silver eyes roamed over Penny. She looked so small and sexy with her magnificent blonde hair falling around her shoulders, her slender body swamped in his robe. He wanted to sweep her into his arms and take her back to bed. But he had to leave soon. 'Yes, I have to go to Mexico on business. Some property I own needs checking. I'd ask you to go with me but I don't think you would enjoy the flight,' he teased.

Penny smiled back at him, a smile that never reached her gorgeous eyes. 'You've got that right. Have a nice trip. I have some work to do,' and she shoved past him and out of the room.

Solo stood frozen to the spot for a second, then, grabbing a towel from the bathroom, he dashed after her, wrapping the towel around his hips as he went. He caught her just before she reached her old bedroom, grasping her by the wrist and spinning her around to face him. 'Now, what the hell was that about?' he demanded angrily. 'Have a nice trip—I thought after last night—'

'You thought what?' Penny cut in. 'That you would indulge your enormous sexual appetite quickly before you left.' Or before Tina arrived, was what she should have said, but the thought angered her too much. 'Well, forget it, buster.'

'I am not going to stand here and argue with you in the hall,' Solo declared icily, straightening to his full commanding height, glacial grey eyes pinned to her flushed and furious face. 'I don't know what's got into you this morning.'

'Not you, that's for sure,' Penny snapped back, and before Solo could respond James came running out of his room.

'Is it time for breakie?'

Breakfast was a tense affair; only the childish chatter of James disguised the silence between the two adults. Then Solo disappeared into the study, and Penny thought things could not get much worse, but they did.

Feeling like death, dressed in jeans and an old blouse and with James at her heels, Penny answered the front door mid-morning to find Tina Jenson smiling down at her.

'Hi, Penny. Solo is expecting me.'

Elegant in a smart grey suit, the skirt ending inches above her knees and revealing her long legs to the best advantage, she walked past Penny.

'Hi,' Penny mouthed automatically in shock and, closing the door, turned to see Solo exit the study, smile at Tina and take the other woman in his arms and plant a kiss on her lips.

Penny stood frozen, her eyes burning in their sockets. She was horribly conscious of her own inadequacy in comparison to the stunning Tina. Her stomach cramped with nausea, which she was pretty sure had nothing to do with her pregnancy.

'Solo's kissing the lady,' James piped up. 'She his wife as well, Penny?'

Out of the mouths of babes, Penny thought bitterly, glancing down at her brother, and murmuring under her breath, 'she is somebody's wife.'

'Penny.' Her name was a command. Penny jerked her head up, her startled gaze clashing with Solo's. 'I have to leave in an hour, and Tina and I have a lot to get through, so could you ask Brownie to serve coffee for two in the study?'

Bitterness turned to fury. Who the hell did he think he was talking to, the patronising pig? Grabbing James's hand, she opened the door. 'Sorry, darling, we are on our way to playschool and already late,' she lied. 'Have a good trip.'

Never in her life had she felt more hurt and humiliated, and, legs trembling, she almost dragged James outside. It was a beautiful June day, but it could have been raining cats and dogs for all Penny cared. She had never dreamt Solo could be so cruel as to bring Tina to her home, and kiss the woman in full view of her and James.

'Come on, James,' she said, tears welling up in her eyes. 'You and I are going for a walk.'

'Nice car.' James pointed to the blue sports car parked behind Solo's BMW.

Penny didn't have a violent bone in her body, but in an action totally out of character she kicked the car as she led James past it and wished it were Tina's bum or, better still, Solo's head…

Carrying a very tired James in her arms, Penny trudged back into the house five hours later.

'Where on earth have you been?' Brownie demanded. 'Poor Solo had to leave without being able to say goodbye. As it was he changed the time-slot for the take-off of his plane twice, but he could not wait any longer.'

Penny put James down on a chair, and then glanced across the kitchen at Brownie. 'There is nothing poor about Solo,' she said. 'And we had lunch at the vicarage, but I could do with a coffee.'

'Sit down and I'll see to it, you look all in.' The concern in Brownie's eyes made Penny want to cry. 'Are you sure you are all right? I could put off going on holiday tomorrow, and wait until Solo returns if you need me.'

'No, no, I'm fine,' Penny said quickly. Religiously every year Brownie and her friend spent the last two weeks in June on holiday in the Lake District and Penny had no wish to spoil Brownie's pleasure. 'Don't worry, just make sure you're packed, and I'll make sure I get the pair of you to the railway station to-morrow to catch your train.'

Penny went up to bed that night, and, lying in the huge bed that not twenty-four hours ago she had shared with Solo, she did cry. The tears trickled down her cheeks. She buried her face in the pillow, but the faint scent of Solo lingered on the fabric and she sobbed all the more. She felt as if her heart would break. She missed him with every breath she took, and she despised herself for loving him, still wanting him, when he had made it plain he did not feel the same.

A long time later, all cried out and tossing and turning in the huge bed, going over every nuance of her relationship with her arrogant husband, she finally realised Solo didn't feel at all.

He was a self-declared loner. From an early age his emotions had been frozen in stone. He had never had anyone, and he didn't need anyone. He was a law unto himself. Wealth and power and striking good looks had enabled him to go through life taking his pick of anything, be it a work of art or a woman, and he cared no more for one than the other.

With that sobering realisation, she also conceded sadly he was not capable of love. Tina might be the nearest he ever got to the emotion, but even that was false. Because a man of his wealth could have arranged for Tina to be divorced and married her years ago if he had really wanted to. Penny could almost feel sorry for Tina—she had worked for him for years and been a convenient body in his bed. Probably still was.

So what did that say about her marriage? Solo had never pretended their marriage was to be a long-term arrangement, and Penny expected it to be over sooner rather than later. Tina was in Central America with him now...

Penny loved Solo, but, knowing him as she did, she realised once he knew she was pregnant he would never let her go. Given his upbringing, he would move heaven and earth to make sure any child of his had what Solo saw as the perfect family: two parents and the best money could buy. It would never enter his head that love was the most essential ingredient, because he had never known it, never felt it, and, as she recalled when he'd demanded she marry him, had freely admitted he did not believe love existed.

Could she stand being married to a man, bearing his child, living with him, loving him, and yet knowing he would never love her? Wondering if he was being unfaithful every moment they were apart...for ever.

No, Penny decided as the early rays of the morning sun slanted across the bedroom. Her stomach rolled and she lay a protective hand across her abdomen. She loved her unborn child and she had more than enough love for two.

Penny washed her mouth out—she had been sick—and looked in the mirror. God, she looked awful, her face was white as a sheet, and she wished she could turn the clock back, and go back to living her old life, the way it had been before Solo had forced her into this impossible position. With her books and only James to take care of, life had been so peaceful.

Maybe she could… The thought that had been festering in her mind all night took root. She was a strong-minded woman, with a growing career—it was time she claimed back her independence.

Penny pulled on a bathrobe and went downstairs. Glancing around the huge hall, she realised she didn't need this house, she didn't need a fortune. In fact, until Solo had made his outrageous proposal she'd been quite resigned to leaving Haversham Park. She was perfectly capable of looking after herself, her brother and her baby.

She must not think of her husband, soon to be her ex. She had made her mind up—she would divorce him for adultery, and to hell with agreements, or pre-nuptials. No more the honourable Penelope, she was going to join the modern, money-grabbing world with a vengeance, she told herself as she set about preparing breakfast for James and Brownie.

It was exactly the right time. As of today Brownie was on holiday. A quick call to Jane in London, and she had no doubt her friend would let her and James stay until she could find somewhere more permanent. As for her arrogant husband, if he tried to get in touch he would find the house empty. He could sweat it out in Mexico with his mistress as long as he liked, as far as Penny was concerned. The longer, the better—it would give her more time to settle into a new life. Solo was a ruthless bastard and she had to stop imagining she loved him.

CHAPTER NINE

SOLO slammed the receiver down, and glanced across the hotel room to where Tina sat sprawled in an armchair. 'Where the hell can she be?' He ran a hand through his hair, and paced the room. 'I've been calling all day every day since I arrived. I rang at night, knowing it was early morning in England, and sure I'd catch Penny before breakfast, or Brownie, even James—someone should have answered. I've called or had someone call for me every hour since, and nothing.'

'You have only been away three days. Why the panic?' Tina asked, watching Solo stride back and forward the length of the sitting room of his hotel suite. 'It's not like you to get ruffled over a lady, even if she is your wife,' Tina couldn't resist teasing him. Solo, her usually coolly controlled, stony-faced boss, now looked anything but. He was definitely cracking up and it had nothing to do with work.

For three days he had dealt with the result of a fire in a luxury block of apartments he owned. Luckily no one had been hurt, but the occupants had been evacuated. But Tina guessed his stress had everything to do with his very beautiful young wife, Penny.

'You don't understand.' Solo walked to the bar and poured a shot of whisky into a crystal glass, and, lifting it to his mouth, he downed it in one gulp, then threw himself down on the sofa. 'You saw how Penny and I parted—she would not even get us a cup of coffee,' he said flatly.

'She was taking her brother to school,' Tina prompted. She did not know Penny well, but she did know Solo had been a lot more hurt than he'd pretended when the girl had finished with him years ago. When she had seen Penny again in Solo's office a few weeks ago, she had been surprised and worried Penny might hurt Solo all over again. It seemed she'd been right.

'No. She didn't have to take James to school, that was just an excuse. Penny was mad at you and me,' Solo opined bluntly. 'Because I let her think we were having an affair.

Why else would I kiss you on the lips when
you arrived?'

'You what?' Tina jerked up in the chair.
'My husband would have something to say
about that, never mind it would be incest.
What on earth possessed you to let your wife
think such a thing? Do you want to lose the
girl?'

'No...I don't know.' Solo rubbed a weary
hand across his eyes. 'Pride, jealousy, anger
or just plain stupidity, I guess.' He looked
across at Tina. 'You might as well know it all.
We didn't break up four years ago because
Penny had another man in her life, but because
a friend of hers that lived in New York had
filled her head with gossip about me, and
scared her off. Including the rumour you were
my mistress.'

'My God!' Tina jumped to her feet. 'The
poor girl thinks you have been having an affair
with me for years.' Moving to sit on the sofa
beside Solo, she reached for his hand, adding,
'You better tell me everything from the beginning.' And he did.

A long time later Tina looked at Solo. 'Let
me get this straight. The first time you met

Penny you decided to marry her because she would make the perfect wife. She said she loved you and then you got the hump when she dumped you because she was scared. The second time around you bullied her into marrying you by threatening her with bankruptcy. Yet the sex is great. That strikes me as odd, and maybe the girl still does care about you. Do you love her?'

Solo reared back. 'I don't believe...' He stopped and nodded. 'Yes.'

'Have you told her?'

'No.'

'And you wonder why she does not answer the phone.' Tina sighed. 'Really, Solo, if you want your marriage to work, if you want to keep Penny, you are going to have to show her you love her, and I don't mean with money or jewels, or even great sex. You have to open your heart, reveal your own pain and insecurities and trust her.'

'It is too late, she has obviously left me to go heaven knows where.' Solo sighed.

'You can appear to be a very cold, intimidating man with your private collection of art as your only company. But a sculpture will not

keep you warm in bed at night, and I know
you're capable of great love. Find Penny and
tell her.' Tina stood up. 'One thing you are not
is a defeatist. I'll have the jet put on stand-by
get washed and get going. I can wrap up here.'

Solo stopped outside the vicarage and looked
up at the house. There was still a light on. He
didn't care if it was after midnight; he had
checked out Haversham Park, and the house
was empty—this was his only hope. The
vicar's daughter was Penny's best friend and
she lived in London. Solo wanted the address
and telephone number.

He hammered on the door, and waited. The
vicar opened the door and Solo demanded to
know where his wife, Brownie or any of his
household was. The vicar insisted Solo have a
drink, told him Brownie was on her annual
holiday. As for Penny and James he had no
idea, but refused to give him Jane's phone
number at this time of night. Late-night calls
were frightening to young women living on
their own.

Solo had to mask a cynical smile. The vicar
obviously was not part of the mobile-phone

and text-message generation. He only parted with the address when Solo gave him his solemn promise he would wait until the morning before driving to London.

Solo returned to the house and the bedroom he had shared with Penny, and spent the early morning hours preparing what he would say to her, and wondering what he would do if Jane didn't know where Penny was and he never found her.

Penny heard the bell ringing, and rolled out of bed. She glanced at the sleeping James on his little camp-bed, and smiled. He thought leaving home was a great adventure, and today because it was Saturday they had planned with Jane to drive out to the zoo.

Slipping on a towelling robe, she tightened the belt and hurried past Jane's bedroom, downstairs and across the hall. It was probably the postman, maybe a parcel as it was Jane's birthday on Monday.

Penny opened the door. She closed her eyes, and opened them again, her heart hammering in her chest. Yes, it wasn't a dream; it was Solo.

'*You.*' she exclaimed, surveying him with wide-eyed amazement. She noted the feverish glitter in his pale eyes that seemed sunken in their sockets, with deep dark circles around them. His black hair fell in rumpled curls over his brow, and he badly needed a shave. His sartorial elegance had deserted him, apparently along with his voice. A tee shirt advertising a certain South American beer hung over his well-worn black jeans.

'What are you doing here?' Penny swallowed hard.

'I could ask you the same question,' Solo replied, and, stepping forward, he reached around her waist, propelling her backwards into the hall, and shut the door behind him. His face expressionless, he looked around the shabby hall. 'Not quite Haversham Park.' Suddenly all his practised speeches deserted him and he was angry. 'What do you think you are playing at? I've been trying to get in touch with you for four days. Where is James?'

Penny pulled free of his restraining arm, and determinedly tightened the belt of her robe. She told herself he was bound to find her sometime. She would have preferred later, rather than sooner. But it did not change her decision one bit. 'James is upstairs in bed, it is barely seven, and I've left you.' She stuck her hands into her pockets, curling them into fists, and lifted her chin. 'And I am not coming back—I want a divorce.' Penny expected him to explode in rage, but he didn't.

Solo's anger deserted him like a spent balloon. His worst fear was realised, and his heart ached as he looked at her. She was wearing a towelling robe, his robe, and it gave him a crumb of hope to know she had taken something of his with her. The over-large lapels were gaping open, revealing the soft swell of her firm breasts. Her magnificent hair was hanging in a tumbled mass down her back. She looked brave and beautiful and incredibly desirable.

His gaze fixed on her luscious mouth, he lifted a hand, and then, taking a deep breath, let it fall to his side. Hauling her into his arms and ravishing her mouth was not an option. She wanted to leave him again... He had taken the one perfect thing in his life and destroyed it, because of his stupid pride, his inability to show the slightest sign of weakness towards anyone.

'Is there somewhere we can talk?' Solo demanded. 'We had an agreement and I deserve an explanation if nothing else,' he said quietly.

Her green eyes narrowed on his. He looked serious, and maybe telling him the truth would be the quickest way to get rid of him. She could still feel the imprint of his hand on her waist and she did not trust herself to spend any length of time in his company without surrendering to his irresistible masculinity all over again.

'Okay, this way,' Penny said, taking charge and, turning, she led him into the little living room. 'You wanted an explanation.' She spun around to face him. 'It is really quite simple. I kept to our agreement, but you did not.' The picture of Tina in his arms, his kissing the other woman, was always there in her head to remind her, and gave her the strength to carry on. 'I was prepared to try and make our marriage work, I gave it my best shot, but when I find my husband kissing his mistress in my own home, even I am not that much of a masochist—'

'No, you've got it wrong,' Solo cut in, reaching out for her and capturing her shoulders. 'I've never been unfaithful. Tina and—'

'No.' Penny flattened her palms on his chest. 'I am not going to listen to any more of your lies.' Just hearing the woman's name on his tongue made her feel sick with jealousy. 'I can't bear to live with a man who is unfaithful.' She lifted glittering green eyes to his. 'Is that clear enough for you?' She tried to shrug free of his hold, but his fingers tightened on her shoulders.

'You're going to listen, damn it,' Solo commanded. He was trying to be humble, but it wasn't easy. 'There is nothing between Tina and I, never has been.'

'Oh, don't give me that,' Penny shot back, her own temper rising. 'I saw you only the other morning on the telephone, and you were aroused simply talking to Tina.'

He stared at her as if she had gone mad; slowly, his mouth turning up in a smile, then a grin, then a chuckle, he shook his dark head. 'Oh, Penny, have you never heard of early-morning arousal in a man; especially this man who happened to be looking at his very lovely wife half naked on the bed? It had nothing to do with Tina.' He folded his arms around her, hauling her hard against his long body. 'And everything to do with you, can't you tell?' His dark head bent and he pressed a kiss to the curve of her neck and shoulder.

Her stomach lurched, the heat of his arousal was hard against her belly, and she shoved at his chest. 'So you say.' She blushed scarlet. 'But I'm not a fool, you are not getting me back with sex.'

Solo stiffened, his arms falling to his sides, and he stepped back, taking a deep, steadying breath. 'No.' His silver eyes captured hers. 'I swore to myself if I found you I would not touch you until I had told you the truth, and the best place to start is probably with Tina.' Penny scowled at the name she hated. 'I promised Tina I would never tell anyone, but there can be no more secrets between us. Tina is my half-sister.'

'Your sister!' Penny exclaimed, her green eyes widening to their fullest extent on his handsome face.

'Yes.' He spoke stiltedly. 'Apparently my mother had a child before me, a baby girl. She sold the child to an Italian-American couple, strictly illegally. Tina's adoptive parents passed her off as their own. She only discovered the truth when she questioned them about the genetic family history when her and her husband discovered she could not have children, and they swore her to secrecy as they are pillars of the community in the small town where they live.'

Penny's head was reeling. The conversation she had heard under the window years ago suddenly made a different sense. Broad-minded about the unconventional family, and of course Solo would always love his half-sister, just as Penny would always love her half-brother. If only she had known! She kept her stunned gaze fixed on Solo's serious face and listened.

'Tina and her husband came to Naples looking for her birth mother, and found me. I was twenty-five at the time and agreed to keep the secret for the sake of her parents. But I can assure you she is very happily married, and enjoys her work.'

Solo lifted his hand and brushed a strand of hair from her cheek. 'I let you think we were

lovers to make you jealous. That's how desperate I was, Penny.' His expression was
bleak.

Penny cleared her throat. 'Desperate for
what?' she made herself ask, the tiniest flame
of hope igniting in her heart. Tina was his sister, not his lover. How much more had she got
wrong? She owed it to herself to find out and
this sombre man was like no Solo she recognised. She instinctively placed a hand on his
chest to steady herself, her legs were shaking,
and she could feel his erratic heartbeat beneath
her palm.

'For you,' Solo said huskily. 'I don't want
to lose you again, Penny.'

Penny stared up at him, her heart racing.
The planes and angles of his face were taut
with tension, he looked so hard, and yet so
incredibly desirable to her foolish heart, and
she despaired at her own weakness. 'You mean
you don't want to lose the sex,' she prompted
bitterly.

'That, too.' His eyes sparked with a trace of
his old arrogance. 'But that is not what I
meant. I am sick of all the pretence, all the
time I have wasted,' Solo said, and she

watched in growing wonder as his expression softened, his firm lips quirked at the corners in a wry smile. 'They say confession is good for the soul, and I promised Tina if I found you I would tell you the truth. Will you listen?'

Penny nodded and allowed him to lead her to the sofa. He sat down and pulled her down beside him. She was intrigued and made no objection when he slipped his arm along the back of the sofa, his hand resting lightly on her shoulder, and turned to face her. A vulnerable, unsure Solo was not something she had ever seen before.

'This isn't easy for me, Penny. I am not the sort of man to reveal my feelings to another person. In fact, until I met you I didn't think I had any. I much prefer inanimate objects to people—they are easier to deal with.'

'That is sad,' Penny murmured and was rewarded with a dry smile.

'No. To me it is...was normal. But—' his great body tensed '—to start at the beginning. Your friend Patricia was right about Lisa Brunton in a way. It was in her apartment some months before I met you that I saw a picture in a magazine of Veronica's wedding

to your father. I recognised her because I had
met her on a friend's yacht—she was his girlfriend. But I also saw you.

'Being a chauvinistic Neanderthal, or whatever you want to call it, I was intrigued by the
difference. You looked so beautiful and innocent. You were my fantasy girl, everything a
man could want in a perfect wife.'

A picture in a magazine! Penny was
stunned, but realised sadly that was so like
Solo—the inanimate object!

'Six months later when I bumped into your
father and Veronica, I had no interest in doing
business with them, but I wanted to meet you.
When I walked into your home and saw you
standing with baby James in your arms, I decided then and there to marry you. In my arrogance the first time I kissed you I knew I
could make you want me, and buying a piece
of land off your father was a small price to pay
for a wife.'

Penny glanced at him. 'A bit medieval,' she
opined, and he had the grace to look embarrassed.

'I asked your father's permission to marry
you the last Saturday before we parted, and

quite happily gave him more money as I thought he was going to be my father-in-law. I had to leave in a hurry before I could ask you, as you know.' He slanted her a wry glance. 'Six days later when I returned I signed the deed for half the house your father insisted on giving me while I waited for you to return home.'

'Oh, my God!' Penny sighed. 'I was so wrong. I came back that day after listening to Patricia's gossip,' she said honestly. 'But I was still determined to believe in you, Solo.' Penny did some confessing of her own. 'But I heard you talking to Tina from beneath the window. I heard you say you wanted a malleable wife, and to refurbish the house, and finally you loved her. I ran straight back to the vicarage and let Simon get me out of the mess I was in.'

'You overheard part of a conversation and judged me on that?' Solo shook his head in disgust. 'I didn't stand a chance.' He shot her an angry glance. 'You didn't trust me at all; no wonder you left me.'

'I'm sorry if you were upset,' she murmured.

'Upset didn't begin to cover it. I was gutted and furiously angry. I became half-owner of a house I didn't want and lost the girl I did,' Solo drawled cynically. 'My pride took a hell of a battering that day.'

'But you didn't love me,' Penny said flatly, and that was the bottom line. He had never loved her.

'No, at the time I did not believe in love,' he told her with brutal candour. 'But with hindsight I realise I do.'

'What are you trying to say?' Penny asked softly, holding her breath.

'For a long time I did not...would not admit I loved you.'

Solo had said he loved her, and she couldn't believe it. She studied his dark features, saw the strain in his silver eyes, and her heart swelled with love. 'You mean you...'

'Let me finish,' Solo commanded. 'I practised this all last night when I thought I might never see you again. If I don't say it now I might never have the nerve again.' His piercing gaze seemed to see right into her soul. 'I was angry when you finished with me, and thought it was a trick by you and your father to con money out of me.'

'Oh, no.' Penny cut in. 'I never knew anything about the money. I can't believe my dad could be so greedy.'

'Yes, well, to give your father his due he did get in touch with me, and offered to give back part of the cash, but he also said he thought you were too young for marriage, and I should try again when you finished university.' His sensuous mouth tightened. 'Deep down I agreed with your father. You were very young, so I told him to keep the money, and decided to do just that in three years' time,' he vouched, almost talking to himself.

Penny stirred restlessly. 'So Dad wasn't really being deceitful,' she said softly.

'No.' Solo agreed. 'But I was, I fluctuated between thinking of your family as no better than thieves, and denying I loved you while hoping to get you back. I knew when you finished university and I was preparing to return to England to see you and find out if you were still with Simon.'

That was the second time he had suggested he loved her, and Penny was beginning to believe him. 'Why didn't you tell me all this when we met again?' What she really wanted to ask was why didn't he say he loved her, but she dared not. She had never known Solo to talk so long and openly and she did not want to miss a word.

Solo's hand tightened on her shoulder. 'I had made a big enough fool of myself once over you and I wasn't prepared to do it twice.' The look he gave her was full of self-mockery. 'When I heard of the death of Veronica and your father, I thought you must know I owned half the house—either your father would have told you or after the will was read. It gives me no pleasure to admit in a way I was glad. My ego had taken enough of a beating where you were concerned. Now I thought, Penelope Haversham will have to come to me,' he declared with some of his old arrogance. 'So I waited and waited for you to get in touch and, the longer I waited, the angrier I got.'

'Oh, Solo.' Penny was appalled by the bitterness in his tone.

But if he heard it he gave no sign. 'Until your solicitor finally got in touch with me, and set up a meeting. Then, the night before, I walked into the hotel bar where I was staying and there you were… *Dio*, Penny, the shock of seeing you in the hotel in a red dress—the innocent vision I had cherished in my mind had transformed into a sexy woman with acres of flesh on display.'

'I thought I felt someone watching me,' Penny recalled. 'But it wasn't my dress—it was Jane's and I was dying of embarrassment, and reeling with shock having just discovered your involvement in my home.' Instinctively she placed her hand over Solo's resting on his knee. 'That is not my style at all, believe me.'

Solo looked into her green eyes and what he saw there gave him hope and the strength to admit what he had been skirting around ever since he'd arrived. 'I know, Penny. Though you did look great, I felt sick.' He paused. 'Sick with love for you.'

'You love me.' Her voice trembled.

'*Dio mio*, I thought that was blatantly obvious.' He wrapped his arms around her, his silver eyes glittering down into hers. 'I love you to the depths of my soul now and for ever.' He bent his head, and gently rubbed his lips softly on hers before adding, 'You are my life, my love, and for a man who has never trusted anyone in his life, I am placing my heart in your hands.'

Elation flooded Penny's mind, and her mouth opened eagerly beneath his. His tongue flicked out to explore the moist, dark cavern of her mouth and hungrily she responded. She lifted her arms around his neck, her fingers streaked through his black curly hair, urgently clasping his skull as the kiss went on and on.

Finally they drew apart, needing to breathe. Solo, his silver eyes glittering with an intensity that touched Penny's heart, said, 'And if you will forgive me and come back to me, I swear I'll make you love me or spend the rest of my life trying.' A faint dark colour burnished his high cheekbones.

Penny could feel the tension in his body, and, although passion glazed her huge green eyes, she saw and recognised the vulnerability in Solo's face. He had told her he loved her, he trusted her, but he still wasn't sure of her.

'You won't have to try. I love you,' she admitted with a beautiful smile. Her heart cried for this perfect man, so alone in the world he had never known love. Her husband was a magnificent male animal, and yet he was afraid to reveal his feelings. 'I have loved you since the first moment I saw you,' she declared, and it was there for him to see in the jade eyes blazing into his. 'You have always had my heart, and I'll never doubt you again or leave you again.'

'I don't deserve you,' Solo husked, his silver eyes, suspiciously moist, fused with Penny's, and then he kissed her almost reverently.

A long moment later, curling her fingers in his silky black hair, Penny sighed happily. 'That red dress has a lot to answer for,' she quipped. 'I wish I had kept it, because it got you to admit you love me, and I seem to remember you came to my house the day after I wore it and seduced me.'

Solo slanted her a sardonic look. 'Not really—as I remember you held out your hand and said, *''Come on''.*'

'You know I didn't mean it the way you took it,' Penny shot back, giving a quick tug on his silky curls. Her arrogant husband was back. It was too much to expect for Solo to

stay humble for long, and if she was honest
she preferred him his usual dynamic self.

'Ow. Woman, that hurt,' Solo said, his eyes
glinting devilishly down into hers. 'But maybe
you're right. By then I was so desperate to
have you that nothing could have stopped me.
Almost four years without a woman is hell on
the old libido,' Solo husked, and lowered his
head, stealing her mouth again in a kiss like
no other they had shared before, a kiss of love
and commitment freely given and a promise
for the future.

'I…you…Solo…really?' She was filled
with awe. 'You didn't…'

'Believe it.' He pressed her back against the
sofa. 'I was waiting for you, no one else would
do.' His mouth captured hers again as one
hand slipped under the lapel of her robe, cupping her breast.

Immediately Penny was aching for him, but,
breaking the kiss, she pulled his hand from her
breast and, holding it in her own, she looked
into his eyes. There was something more she
needed to know. 'Then why after we made
love the first time were you so cold, and demanded we marry on a temporary basis?'

'Because I dare not face another rejection.' The look he gave her was full of self-mockery and, lifting her hand to his mouth, he kissed the wedding band on her finger. 'I figured once I got you wearing my ring and in my bed, time was on my side. I thought I had succeeded on our honeymoon, but when we got back to England and I suggested we could travel together and you turned me down flat...' He let go of her hand and curved his own around the back of her neck, holding her face up to his, and looking deep into her green eyes. 'It felt like another rejection, Penny, and I couldn't take any more. I didn't know whether to love you or hate you, all I knew was that you loved that old house a hell of a lot more than me.'

She saw the flash of anguish in his eyes that he could not disguise, and her heart wept for him. This proud, wonderful man, so scared by his childhood, he didn't believe anyone could love him, she realised. 'So that was why you were in a temper. I wondered but I was afraid to ask, because I thought you were already tired of me.' Penny traced the outline of his lips with a loving finger, determined to let him know it was all right to be afraid by revealing her own doubts. Love was a scary emotion, but she had to show him how much she adored him. 'I loved our honeymoon and it was there on the tiny beach I realised I still loved you, Solo. I'd always loved you, and I did not want our marriage to ever end, still don't,' Penny admitted huskily.

Solo looked at her with brilliant eyes. 'You and I both,' he declared in a voice that was not quite steady. 'The last day at the cabin as we were leaving, you said you wanted to return one day. I looked at you, and wiped a tear from your cheek and said no problem, I would drive you across from England any time you wanted. But in my head I thought I would drive you to the ends of the earth if you asked. I was struck dumb. That was the moment, when I finally admitted to myself I loved you, and I was scared.'

Penny closed her arms around his neck and smiled up at him, her eyes shining with love and something else. 'I'm so happy I wasn't just bought and paid for.'

'Never.' Solo lowered his dark head, murmuring huskily, 'I love you as you love me.' He covered her face and throat with tiny kisses. 'And I'm never letting you go again,' he declared adamantly, pulling her onto his lap and kissing her thoroughly.

'I'm afraid you will have to,' Penny suddenly cried, and slid off his lap and dashed for the hall cloakroom.

'Penny, please.' Solo followed her. She couldn't leave him now; she couldn't change her mind. For a second he froze. She was leaning over the toilet bowl being violently sick. Oh, *Dio*! What had he done to her now? 'Penny, *cara*.' He leant over her, placing a supporting hand around her head and another around her waist. 'What's wrong?'

Penny straightened up, washed her mouth out at the vanity basin, and sank back against the hard length of his body. 'I'm fine now for the rest of the day—it only lasts for a couple of minutes.' She felt his arms wrap around her stomach, and smiled at his image in the mirror in front of her. Her stony-faced husband looked sicker than she felt, and she smiled. 'I'm pregnant, we are pregnant.' Suddenly she was lifted up in his arms and carried back to the living room.

'Oh, my God, you better lie down.' Solo deposited her on the sofa and knelt on the floor. 'You're sure?' His silver eyes glistened 'When, how?'

A mischievous smile parted her full lips and, rising up, she pulled Solo up onto the sofa beside her. No longer shy but all sensuous woman, with a slender hand she traced the outline of firm jaw, then trailed one finger down his strong throat and lower to scrape over a cotton-covered, hard male nipple, and she felt his body shudder.

'You know very well how, Solo.' A tiny grin flirted around the edge of her mouth. 'As for the when, probably the first time we made love.'

Powerful hands burrowed under the towelling robe and pulled her close so her naked breast brushed his broad chest. Gleaming silver eyes burnt into hers. 'You have made me the happiest man alive, and the randiest right at this moment.' Solo groaned. His dark head dipped, and his mouth claimed hers as his hand cupped one firm breast.

'Solo, you're here! Are you coming to the zoo?' James asked.

A wave of frustration went through him. Solo quickly adjusted Penny's robe, and crossed his legs. He looked balefully at the little boy standing in the doorway. Then it hit him. Very soon he might have a son of his own. 'James.' He grinned broadly. 'Sorry, but I can't come to the zoo with you today.' Never one to miss a chance, as Jane walked in behind the boy he continued smoothly, 'Penny isn't feeling too well. So I am going to stay and look after her, while you and Jane go to the zoo.'

'Nice try, Solo,' Jane said with a glance at her friend's and her husband's flushed faces, and, guessing exactly what they had been doing, she was glad. 'But Penny is driving.' She grinned.

'No problem,' Solo drawled. 'I'll get the firm's limousine to take you both—it will be much safer that way, and you will have a man to help you around.' His grey eyes gleamed wickedly at Jane. 'The female staff are of the opinion the chauffeur is rather handsome and he's single, Jane, but make sure you bring him back. I'm taking Penny and James home tonight.'

Jane started to laugh. 'I can see why Penn
loves you—you're a devil.'

'Alone at last,' Solo husked, walking toward
Penny.

Breakfast over, Jane and James had left i
the limousine for the zoo.

Penny, showered and dressed in a cotto
print dress, was leaning against the kitche
sink having just finished washing the dishes.

'I thought they were never going to leave
Let's go upstairs.' Penny agreed.

'You really are devious.' Penny gasped a
Solo slipped her dress down over her hips. '
heard you tell the chauffeur not to come bac
until after six, and you'd pay him double.' Sh
grinned up at him, her eyes shining with lov
and something more.

Solo laughed and pulled her into his arms
He had already stripped off, and his perfectl
honed body gleamed golden in the daylight
his silver eyes sparked into hers. 'So I have
lot of time to make up for.'

'You're incorrigible.' Penny planted a kis
on his sensuous mouth, and nibbled on his bot
tom lip as his hands shaped her waist and

thighs and slowly moved back up to remove her bra and cup her full breasts, his thumbs deliberately teasing the rigid, dusky peaks. Penny closed her eyes, breathing deeply as wave after wave of pleasure surged from her breasts to her thighs. Solo's husky-voiced, 'If I don't have you soon I'll die,' had her eyes flying open just as they tumbled back on the bed.

Solo looked into her eyes. He was breathing fast, his own eyes gleaming. 'I love you, Penny,' he said in a deep voice raw with feeling, then his mouth was on hers, hot, hard and insistent.

Penny was swept along on a great tidal wave of desire. They made love with a breathtaking, compelling, frantic urgency, an uninhibited passion that only two people who truly loved could claim. They possessed each other. As morning turned to afternoon the only sounds in the room were the murmured endearments, heavy breathing, the occasional laughter and the hoarse cries of completion.

Finally they clung together, sated and exhausted for the moment. Penny sighed. 'You really don't mind that I am pregnant?'

Solo leaned over her, tipped up her chin with a finger and kissed her, and it was some time later before he answered her question. He said unsteadily, 'I'm thrilled.'

'But how...how could it happen? How could they not know?' Solo demanded, looking tense and anxiously down into Penny's sparkling green eyes. 'The doctor, I mean... The hospital... I paid for the best...'

Propped up in the bed in the master bedroom of their Italian home, Penny bit her lip to stop from laughing. Ever since she had given birth suddenly twenty-four hours ago and three weeks early in this very bed, Solo had hardly left her except to pace to the two cribs and stare. His legendary cool control had completely deserted him.

'I seem to remember...' she lifted a slender hand and ran it teasingly up his long thigh '...it had something to do with a "come on" and you.'

'You know what I mean...' Solo began, and paused, catching her hand on his thigh and sinking down to sit on the bed, his handsome features relaxing in a wry, if tired smile. 'But wins, a boy and a girl, my darling, Paulo and Tina,' he husked in wonder.

He had flatly refused to call the boy Solo, but had agreed to Paulo. In fact he had felt like Saul on the road to Damascus, redeemed by the love of Penny over the past seven months. She was his life. Solo rarely travelled on business any more; he delegated. They split their time between England and Italy. James was like a son to him, and now this…

'The best room was booked, I had it all arranged.' He still had trouble getting his head around it. The shock of seeing Penny in pain, and his housekeeper deliver the baby boy, had hurt and then awed him, his heart flooding with love for the tiny infant. But ten minutes later when the girl had appeared he had fainted. That the doctor had eventually arrived and declared everything was fine had done nothing to dispel his shock.

He lifted Penny's hand to his mouth and pressed kisses to her palm, and then raised his head and gave her a serious look. 'That's it; we are never doing this again,' he commanded forcibly. 'I can't bear to see you in pain.'

Penny felt the ripples of excitement in her palm, and grinned. 'No more sex, then.' She chuckled at the sudden flash of panic in his silver eyes.

'Witch.' His lips curved in a sensuous smile.

'You know what I mean.' Leaning forward, he captured her mouth in a deep, devouring kiss.

'Yes, all your money and planning gone to pot,' she teased when she had got her breath back. She was so happy she could burst. 'And I don't know what you are complaining about,' she added with a beaming smile, looking up into his incredible silver eyes. 'After all, you got the deal of the day. Two for the price of one!'

'I got the deal of a lifetime and beyond when I got you, Penny.' Solo blinked the moisture from his eyes, and gathered her into his arms. 'You have given me the greatest gift in our two perfect babies. I love you. You're my love, my wife, my life.'

With a heart brimming over with love and happiness, Penny stared at him, too full to speak, but she didn't need to. Glittering silver meshed with misty green and the look they exchanged said it all...